GRAVE MISCONDUCT

EVA CHASE

GANG OF GHOULS

BOOK
3

Grave Misconduct

Book 3 in the Gang of Ghouls series

First Digital Edition, 2022

Copyright © 2022 Eva Chase

Cover design: Yocla Book Cover Design

Ebook ISBN: 978-1-990338-40-3

Paperback ISBN: 978-1-990338-31-1

ONE

Lily

It was probably kind of ridiculous to be wandering the streets shouting, "Marisol!" every few seconds, like my sister would come running to me if she heard her name. Like she hadn't purposefully run *away* from me an hour ago, yelling at me to leave her alone. Really, it might have made more sense to shut up so she didn't know I was coming.

But without any idea where she'd run off to, it wasn't as if I could sneak up on her anyway. I couldn't help hoping that whatever magical delusion had come over her to make her think that I was the enemy, it'd fade away, and she'd want to come back.

She'd dashed out of my apartment in nothing but

her pajamas, not even slippers on her feet. Even at midday, the fall air was getting nippy, and the city streets in Mayfield weren't exactly meant for barefoot frolicking. I was a little chilled, and that was after Nox had gone back to the apartment to get my housecoat and proper shoes.

"Marisol!" I called again, peering down a dingy alley.

A stray cat hissed at me and raced off between the dumpsters. My panic and frustration thrummed more frantically in my chest. In response, without my intending it, a jet of water shot from a nearby storm drain. It spouted ten feet in the air before splattering back to the ground.

It didn't know how to find my sister either.

I couldn't say that it'd drawn more attention to me than I'd already gotten, though. My apartment was in an up-and-coming neighborhood that was still working on the whole coming part, and I'd ventured into an area that was still pretty down. All the same, there weren't a whole lot of people wandering around in pajamas and a housecoat hollering someone's name, while nearby water sources periodically splashed and splattered like they had a mind of their own.

Oh, and the herd of frogs that'd gathered behind me would have accounted for a lot of the stares I was getting from bystanders too.

I glanced down at my feet. During the hour I'd been searching, more and more desperate energy racing through my body without any real target to direct it at,

I'd amassed a small army of about fifty of the eager amphibians. They hopped across the sidewalk, some of them peering up at me as if waiting for my command, others leaping ahead like they thought they might be able to track down my sister on their own. Unfortunately, they didn't seem to be much use as bloodhounds.

"You should go back to the marsh or wherever you came from," I murmured at them from the corner of my mouth. I wasn't so frantic that I couldn't figure out I'd look even more unhinged if it was obvious I was carrying on a conversation with my froggy friends. "You're going to end up roadkill around here." I'd already seen one smashed under a tire during my search.

The frogs kept hopping around, somewhat aimlessly other than their determination to stick with me. I guessed I should appreciate their loyalty even if they were kind of useless. It wasn't like *I* was being of much use to anyone at the moment.

I glanced at the grubby buildings and cracked pavement around me once more and pulled out my phone. For approximately the millionth time, I dialed Marisol's number.

Her cell phone immediately clicked over to voicemail. As her awkward teenage voice announced who I'd reached, I debated leaving a message, but she already had ten or so from me. I didn't really have anything to add at this point.

If I'd known the magic words to bring her back, I'd have said them in the first place.

I wasn't even totally sure she had her phone on her. Most teenagers seemed to be glued to the things, but she might have left it in her bag at my apartment, like she had so much else. I hadn't gone back to check.

As I sighed and shoved the phone into my housecoat's plush pocket, Kai came trotting over from a nearby street. He took in my motion and expression, and his gray-green eyes darkened behind the rectangular panes of his glasses. "Still no answer, huh?"

I shook my head, and he dodged the frogs as he reached to squeeze my shoulder. Kai wasn't really a PDA kind of guy, even though I'd found out just how enthusiastic he could be in private, so that gesture was the equivalent to him sweeping me into a hug.

Speaking of which...

Ruin loped over from a different direction, caught sight of my face, and immediately wrapped his well-muscled arms around me in one of his epic embraces. "We'll find her, Angelfish," he assured me, nuzzling my hair. "With all of us looking, we've got to."

Kai frowned. "I'd imagine if she was somewhere easily locatable in the area, we'd have stumbled on her by now. Maybe it's time to change tactics."

"No sign of her down that way," Jett said, joining us with a jerk of his thumb over his shoulder in the direction he'd come from.

"I couldn't find a trace of her," Nox agreed as he walked over. He cracked his knuckles, looking taller and brawnier than ever in the professor body he'd recently

4

taken over and made his own. "None of the people I *pressed* for information had seen her either."

I wasn't going to ask exactly how he'd "pressed" them. I didn't see any blood on his hands, so he couldn't have done that much damage.

I pinched the bridge of my nose. "We can't leave her running around the city on her own. She doesn't have proper clothes—she doesn't have money—I don't think she's ever even been in Mayfield before!"

Kai cocked his head. "She might not be on her own. You think her outburst was triggered by Nolan Gauntt's magic, right? He might not have only been driving her away from you."

A lump rose in my throat. "You mean he might have been bringing her to him." And what would the uber-powerful business magnate who we'd only recently discovered had unknown amounts of voodoo powers do with her?

Jett raked his fingers through the scruffy hair he'd dyed a deep purple, a far cry from his straightlaced nerd host's previous preppy style. "So we go after him. Easy."

"Not easy," I said, my heart sinking. "We don't know what he's capable of. We're not prepared to go up against him. I threw a bunch of my water magic at him before, and he only laughed."

At the anguish that came with the admission, a sink faucet by a nearby window started sputtering in distress. Several of the frogs croaked in a gloomy chorus. I dragged in a breath and did my best to tamp down on the unsettled energies reverberating through me.

Nox drew himself up to his full, substantial height, the sunlight catching off the red tips of his spiky black hair and making them glow like little flames. "We're not giving up," he said firmly. "We're just regrouping for a more concentrated attack, if that's what we need to do. Let's go back to the apartment, and we can figure out exactly what we've got to work with." He narrowed his eyes, glancing around us. "For all we know, he's got spies out here."

I didn't really want to leave off the search, but I had to admit it'd been hopeless so far. How would it help Marisol to keep roaming around like a crazy woman when maybe we could figure out something better? Gritting my teeth, I nodded.

We trudged toward the apartment, Ruin keeping his arm around me, stroking reassuring fingers up and down my side. Partway there, Kai took out his own phone. "I could try to get in touch with Nolan himself. I haven't been able to get his direct number, but I have his admin assistant's and various other people at Thrivewell."

From the time he'd spent working at the Gauntts' corporate head office. He'd gotten much closer to the upper echelon than I had in my brief mailroom stint. But his proposal brought a flare of panic back into my chest.

"No," I said quickly. "You'll blow your cover. As far as we know, he hasn't found out that there's anyone else connected to me working at Thrivewell. We might need you to go back in on Monday and scope things out from inside the office."

"Good point." He snapped his deft fingers. "I'll give *you* the assistant's number. Nolan obviously called your sister away for a reason. He might want to lord it over you."

I didn't like the idea of hearing my nemesis gloating about how he'd brainwashed Marisol, but I could put up with it if it meant he might spill the beans about more of his plans in typical supervillain style. Unfortunately, when I dialed the number Kai gave me, the phone on the other end didn't even ring. All I got was a digitized female voice informing me, "Sorry, your call could not go through as dialed."

I scowled at the phone and tried again in case I'd tapped the wrong number, but I got the same result. Nox growled under his breath. "The bastard already blocked you. I guess he isn't a gloater."

Maybe that wasn't surprising. We'd found my resume in Nolan's desk—he'd known my main phone number.

"You could get a burner phone and try from a number he won't recognize," Ruin suggested cheerfully. "Sneak past his defenses."

"If he's blocked me, then he isn't going to take any calls from me even if I use the president's phone number," I grumbled. "Not that I can get that."

Kai's gaze went briefly distant. "If I talked to the right people… But it's true. If he doesn't want to talk, he won't talk. Unless we make him." The fierce light that only came into his eyes when he was particularly fired up flashed behind his glasses.

"Oh, we'll make him, all right," Nox muttered. "That pompous prick's ass is toast."

When we came into the apartment, my heart lurched all over again. The plate from Marisol's pancakes was still sitting on the dining table, sticky with syrup. She'd left her hoodie draped over the back of the sofa. I could sense her presence in the space even though she wasn't here now.

In the bathroom, the shower started spewing water in jerky spurts. The frogs who'd followed us upstairs bounded over to have a little bathtub party or something. I sank into the chair next to my own abandoned plate.

Ruin sat next to me, pulling his chair close, and Jett wandered through the room with a pensive expression. It was hard to tell whether the gangster artist was picturing how he'd destroy our enemies or how he'd like to give the room another makeover. Kai stood at my other side, resting his hands on the back of a chair. Nox paced back and forth with a frustrated air that echoed the energy churning inside me.

"What exactly did she say and do?" he asked me. "How did you know it was the Gauntt guy affecting her?"

I squared my shoulders and forced myself to replay the events of this morning in my head. "We were eating pancakes for breakfast right here." I motioned to the plates. "You texted me asking about coming over to meet her. I was about to tell her a little more about the four of you. Then all of a sudden, she jumped up and started accusing me of dragging her away from her family... of acting crazy... She said she couldn't trust me and she didn't want to be around me."

Tears pricked at the backs of my eyes. I'd thought I'd figured that one problem out—I'd gotten my sister away from our mom and stepdad, who'd treated both of us like dirt under their shoes. I'd found this apartment where she had a room of her own, set her up with drawing supplies so she could dig back into her art, and reached out to a nearby high school to work out a transfer.

But the problem wasn't that I hadn't done enough. She'd been happy until that weird spell had gripped her.

I forced myself to keep talking. "She ran for the door. I tried to stop her, because it was obvious something wasn't right. I grabbed her arm, and her pajama top tore—I saw a mark on the underside of her arm." I touched my own arm where I'd had a similar birthmark-like blotch, about the size of a nickel, just beneath my armpit until I'd walked into the marsh yesterday and managed to break Nolan's spell that'd blocked off my memories of finding him with her.

I'd felt so powerful in that moment. Like I could conquer anything he threw at me next. I hadn't had any idea he'd throw this big a pile of shit down on me.

Kai motioned to my arm. "You said you had a mark from when he used his magic on you—that it disappeared after you got back your memories. How similar was the one on your sister's arm?"

"I only saw it for a second." I paused, straining to remember. "It was almost exactly the same size and really close to the same spot, pink, a few shades darker than the rest of her skin. The shape was a little different, but overall fairly round like mine."

"Wait a second!" Ruin groped at his pockets for his phone and started flipping through photos. Then he held up the screen with a triumphant grin. "Look."

At first, all I could see was the fact that it was a naked woman. A naked woman I happened to know. That phone had once belonged to Ruin's host, a jerk named Ansel, and it looked like Peyton, one of my bullies at college who'd had her eyes on Ansel, had been sending him nudes as part of her attempted seduction. This picture showed her from the waist up, totally bare, sprawled out with one arm tucked behind her head and her other hand playing with her lips.

"Ruin," Nox snarled, "I don't think that's the kind of thing you should be showing off around our—"

"No!" I said, my gaze catching on the detail that'd obviously excited Ruin. "He's right. She's got a mark just like mine and Marisol's."

I grabbed the phone and zoomed in the picture, both to get a closer look and so we didn't have perky nipples staring back at us while we studied the image. The details blurred a bit, but the lighting was good enough that the birthmark was still obvious.

"That," I said, pointing at the pink mark with its

slightly mottled edges. "That's almost exactly what it looked like." My forehead furrowed. "Why would Peyton have one too?"

Kai had leaned in, studying the picture intently. He turned to Ruin. "Did your boy Ansel get nudes from anyone else?"

"I dunno," Ruin said. "I just flipped by those the other day when I was checking to see if there was anything in here that'd tell us who'd be after him, but I didn't go very far back. Let me check. There could be!"

He started skimming through the photo album in what was now The Great Nudes Search. He hadn't gotten all that far before he gave a little cry of victory. I braced myself for more boobs, but instead he held up a picture of Ansel posing in a Speedo that left nothing to the imagination.

My first thought was that I vastly preferred the slight softness Ruin's possession had brought to all those hard ridges of muscle. My second was that Ansel had an interesting-looking little splotch on the underside of his arm, a little lower down than the others, about halfway between his elbow and armpit.

"Do you still have that?" Jett asked from where he'd come over to join the discussion properly.

Ruin tugged the sleeve of his Henley up to his shoulder and checked. His skin was smooth and unmarked with its fading summer tan. "Nope. I guess the voodoo broke when I took over."

"Let me see." Nox made a grabby gesture at the phone. When Ruin handed it over, he zoomed in, squinting at the image. His square jaw worked. "I think… I think one of those bozos who hauled Lily out to the docks might have had something like that too."

He raised his head to meet my eyes. "Maybe your bullies weren't just jackasses. Maybe they were Nolan Gauntt's puppets."

two

Lily

Finding out that Peyton might have had reasons for harassing me beyond being a raging bitch didn't make me all that more eager to talk to her. I mean, the girl had pushed me down a flight of stairs, locked me in a lecture hall's utility room, helped a bunch of other students set me up to get fired from my job and maybe arrested, threatened to drown me in a toilet bowl…

Maybe Nolan had brainwashed her into acting out in particularly extreme ways, but it was hard to believe she'd been all that kindly a soul to begin with.

We started with her anyway, because we also knew enough about her to figure out where she lived. We didn't even know the guy from the dock's first name.

Along with the various pictures she'd texted Ansel—which he'd obviously saved even though it didn't seem he'd ever had any intention of using her as more than fapping material, leaving me with even fewer regrets about his death—she'd told him her room number in the college residence building "in case you ever want to stop by."

When we reached the campus, Kai and Jett went off to see what they could find out about the dock guy, and Nox and Ruin joined me in heading over to Peyton's dorm. It was after most classes would have ended but before people would be heading out for evening entertainment, so we figured we had a pretty good chance of catching her there. Ruin was joining in since she still saw him as Ansel, regardless of dyed scarlet hair, softened features, and sunny new disposition. Nox wanted to be sure she didn't throw me down any more stairs.

"I should rearrange her face for everything she did to you already," he muttered as we headed up the stairs.

"Somehow I think that'll make her less likely to talk rather than more," I pointed out, and paused to scoop up one of the few frogs that'd insisted on joining me in the car for the trip over here. "Anyway, I already put the fear of the marsh into her. I don't think she's going to risk another frog attack."

Nox scoffed. "It'll be more than frogs coming at her if she takes a jab at you. I'll hang her out to dry."

Ruin was busy strategizing as he bounded up the stairs. "I could thank her for the pictures—tell her I was

14

looking at them again and noticed her birthmark—maybe she could let us take a look at it in person—"

"Um, no, let's not lead with asking her to get undressed," I said. Even though she might have done it for the guy she thought was Ansel. But I wasn't leaving her alone with Ruin to find out how far she'd try to take her efforts. "I don't think we should talk about the pictures at all. We'll just ask her about the Gauntts and see how she reacts."

"Perfect!" Ruin said cheerfully, never one to be fazed by having his plans shot down.

I tucked the frog I was holding close to my side as we navigated down the busy residence hallway. When we knocked on Peyton's door, no one answered. She and her roommate had a whiteboard tacked to the outside, on which several guys had left propositions directed at one or both of them. These ranged from the very smooth, *DTF? Call me!* to the almost poetic *Bring your P to ride my D, girl.*

And now I was even more glad I'd never attempted to live on campus.

We stood there for a few minutes, getting odd looks from some of the students who passed by, at least a few of whom might have recognized Nox as the former Professor Grimes, even with his makeover. I stroked my thumb over the frog's sleek back and debated leaving a little note of my own. But what was I going to say? *Hey Pey, wanna give it up for me? And by "it" I mean all the dirt about what Nolan Gauntt did to you.*

Yeah, I didn't think that'd go over super well.

I turned to go and spotted the girl we'd been waiting for heading toward us through the hall. Peyton saw me at the exact same moment, her willowy frame tensing. I'd swear even across the several feet between us, her gaze shot straight to the frog in my hand, and she went a little green herself.

Then her eyes landed on Ruin. She slowed, looking torn between running in the opposite direction and throwing herself at him. She settled for coming to a halt just out of arm's reach and hugging herself. She glanced at Ruin. "Hi, Ansel. I wish you'd come on your own."

Ruin beamed at her. "We all had something to talk to you about."

Nox jabbed his thumb toward the door. "Let's get out of the hall so the whole world doesn't know our business."

Peyton eyed me skeptically. "I don't want to go anywhere with *her*."

As if I'd done half the damage to her friends that the guys had. But she'd fled the scene at the grocery store—she'd never seen them fully in action firsthand. And her crush on Ansel had obviously given her rose-tinted glasses so thick it was amazing she wasn't walking into walls.

I tucked the frog into my pocket. "I promise I won't call my friends down on you as long as you keep your hands to yourself."

Peyton let out a little huff, but when Ruin tilted his head to the side and said, "Please?" she gave in and unlocked the door.

It was barely big enough for the four of us to squeeze inside between the two beds. Peyton perched on the edge of her tiny desk and narrowed her eyes at us, letting them soften only briefly when they passed over Ruin. "What's going on? What do you want?"

She couldn't seem to decide whether to sound concerned or hostile. Seeing me and Ruin together was clearly throwing her for a loop, even though she'd known he'd been hanging out with me.

Suddenly I had no idea how to start this conversation. For all intents and purposes, I was about to ask her if a creepy old man had molested her as a child. That was kind of a difficult subject to lead with.

At least, in my mind it was. My guys clearly didn't have the same qualms.

"Has anything happened between you and Nolan Gauntt?" Nox said while I hesitated. "Now or when you were a kid?"

Ruin nodded and clarified, "Weird stuff? Did he touch you?"

Peyton's jaw dropped open in an expression of horror, and I had the urge to bury my face in my hands. Sensitive, the Skullbreakers' approach was not.

"What are you talking about?" she sputtered, recoiling farther back on the desk as if *we'd* been trying to grope her. "I wouldn't—a guy like him wouldn't— You're *sick*."

"Whoa," I said, holding up my hands as I tried to salvage the conversation. "We're not accusing you of anything. We're just... worried." And maybe I needed

17

to bring up her body parts after all. "We found out some... other people he's messed with had these little marks on their arm, and we noticed you have one too. Right here?" I prodded the spot on my own arm. "You do have a birthmark kind of thing there, right? Do you remember how you got it?"

Peyton's face twitched. She grasped her arm, and I could tell from her expression that she knew what mark I meant. But she shook her head vehemently. "Lots of people have birthmarks. It's been there since I was a kid. It doesn't have anything to do with anyone. No one *put* it there. You really are psycho."

My jaw clenched at the familiar insult. It was pretty debatable which of us had actually acted more psycho in the past month.

Nox growled and loomed closer, and I grabbed him before Peyton had to do more than squeak in fear.

"It's fine," I told him. "I'm embracing my crazy." Then I turned back to her. "You're sure you've had that mark since you were a kid?"

"Yeah," Peyton said in an increasingly crabby tone. She hugged herself tighter. "These things don't just appear out of nowhere."

"Sometimes they do," Ruin said, ever so helpfully, but at least he followed it up with a useful question. "Did you have anything to do with the Gauntts when you were a kid?"

"You obviously know who Nolan Gauntt *is*," Nox growled.

Peyton glowered at him. "Of course I do. Everyone

does. My mom works for Thrivewell. I'm sure he came to a few dinners at the house, or there were Christmas parties or something. But he didn't put a freaking *birthmark* on my arm."

Not that she remembered. My gut twisted. Nolan had made me forget what I'd seen and Marisol forget that he'd done anything more than talk briefly with her. And he hadn't marked her while I'd been there—he must have seen her again, later. God, how many times had he been alone with my sister after I'd been shipped off to the looney bin?

An icy chill passed through me, but I yanked my mind back to the present. Getting these answers would help me figure out that part—as well as how to find Marisol now.

"There might be things you don't remember," I said. "But maybe I could… jog your memory. If you'd let me try." I reached for her arm, thinking of how I'd shattered the supernatural wall inside my own mind and body with my powers.

Peyton jerked away, her posture going even more rigid. "Get away from me! You're all fucking crazy. Get out of my room." She paused, looking at Ruin for a moment. "I don't know why you're letting them drag you into this, but it's too much. Just get out."

"We only wanted to help," Ruin protested.

Peyton stood up on the chair by the desk. "Get out *now* or I'm going to scream at the top of my lungs. And tell everyone who comes that *you* creeps were 'touching' me."

Nox bared his teeth and moved as if to lunge at her, but I pushed in front of him. "It's not worth it," I said, even though my heart was sinking. "If she won't cooperate, we can't force it. Let's just go."

Nox might have tried to force the issue regardless, but right then his phone pinged with a text. He checked it, and his shoulders relaxed a bit. "Kai came through. We have a plan B."

I opened my mouth, thinking maybe I should clarify in front of Peyton that he didn't mean *that* Plan B, but then I decided trying to tell her more about what was going on here would only make her more likely to scream. She could come up with whatever theories she wanted about what he was talking about. I didn't give a shit.

"Okay," I said. "Where should we meet him and Jett?"

We left Peyton silently behind, closing her dorm-room door behind us. Nox led the way out through the residence building and across campus.

We found Kai, Jett, and the broad-shouldered, snub-nosed guy who'd stuffed me in his trunk a few weeks ago at the edge of the campus parking lot. The guy was sitting on the ground with his back against a tree, his face sallow. When he saw us approaching, he started to whimper.

"Just leave me alone," he said, pulling his knees up to his chest and rocking back and forth. "I'm not going anywhere near her again. You've got to give me a break now."

He looked like he was already on the verge of a mental breakdown. I guessed that was a reasonable response to the Skullbreakers' brand of ghostly gangster justice. The last time he'd seen Nox, Nox had punctured his face with a handful of fishhooks. I could see the little dots on his cheeks where the wounds hadn't quite finished healing.

And it looked like Kai and Jett had been manhandling him already. The sleeve of the guy's shirt was torn as if one of them had wrenched it too hard in a tussle to roll it up.

"He's got that mark thing," Jett reported.

"He claims it's been there since he was 'little,'" Kai added to Jett's typically brusque report. "And that all he knows about Nolan Gauntt is that the guy came by to talk to him about college scholarships back when he was in elementary school." He raised a skeptical eyebrow.

"That *is* all I know," the bully whined. "Please, don't hurt me again."

He was so pathetic I couldn't help pitying him a little. He'd been a shit to me just like Peyton had, but at least he had the sense to realize he'd screwed up and that he should cut out the shit from here on.

"I can try to break any blocks on his memory like I did with my own," I said, and crouched down across from the guy.

He cringed away, folding his arms close to his chest. I didn't like the idea of forcing him either. As I considered my options, Ruin dove down beside me.

21

"I can help!" he said brightly. "There's nothing to worry about here."

He said that second bit while he was punching the guy in the chest. Which might have contradicted his words, except the punch came with a little crackle of supernatural energy, and suddenly our target was smiling back at us.

"You're right," he said. "I don't know why I was so scared. It's good to see you guys."

Nox snorted and shook his head in bemusement. All of the guys' ghostly energies had been taking on their own unique edge, and Ruin's angle was infecting others with emotions.

It was helpful, though. "What's your name?" I asked the guy, because I wanted to at least know that much about who we were dealing with.

"Fergus," he said easily.

Well, now that the issue had already been forced despite my intentions, it seemed better to do what I could for him rather than leave him in the dark.

"Okay, Fergus," I said like I was talking to a small child. "I'm just going to check out your arm for a minute. I think there might be something a little wrong with it, and I'm going to fix it."

"That's great," Fergus said, smiling away. "Thank you for helping me."

It was even more unnerving seeing him all mellow after his previous terror. I tugged up his sleeve and immediately spotted the birthmark a few inches above his elbow. Readying myself, I wrapped my hands around his bicep.

A hum of tension was still reverberating through me from my distress over Marisol's disappearance. I clicked my tongue against the roof of my mouth, setting a quiet rhythm to go with the thump of my pulse and the rustle of the breeze through the leaves on the branches overhead, and focused my mind.

Nolan Gauntt. This was all about him. He'd cozied up to my sister in totally inappropriate ways—he'd done who knew what to the guy in front of me. The asshat could be putting his hands all over Marisol right now.

I winced inwardly at the image, and my anger and fear roared up inside me, driving the hum to more potency. A tingling sensation spread through my arms to my hands. I closed my eyes.

It was there. Like a storm break, a barrier inside Fergus's flesh that stretched all the way into his mind. I trained all my attention on it, summoning the imaginary waves that I'd used to batter down the wall inside me. Then I threw them at it over and over again like watery punches.

This was for stealing my sister away. *This* was for messing around with who knew how many other kids. *This* was for laughing in my face when I'd challenged him. *This* was for having me shut away in a psych hospital for seven years of my life.

With each punch, I hit harder. Then I threw everything I had at the mark and the barrier emanating from it with one last surge of horror.

The impression of the wall fractured and crumbled away. I let go of Fergus, gasping a breath as I came back to the world around me.

Fergus was staring down at his arm. Then he gaped at all of us. His face had gotten its usual color back after Ruin had calmed him down, but now a sickly hue rolled over it again.

"Nolan Gauntt," he murmured, with a shiver that shook his whole body.

three

Ruin

"You remember!" I said eagerly, grinning at the guy Lily had just worked her powers on. It was obvious from the dude's expression that he hadn't remembered anything all that *good*, but really, anything *was* good for our purposes. We just needed to find out what he knew.

As Lily eased back a step, staying crouched in front of the guy, I turned my smile on her. It really was something to watch her put her powers to use. I had no idea how exactly she was breaking Nolan Gauntt's magic, but the energy inside her radiated out into the air when she concentrated like that. It'd sent an unearthly quiver over my skin that reminded me of all the other sensations our woman could stir up in me.

What an amazing woman she was. We'd get her sister back, because I knew there wasn't any chance of her backing down. And the four of us would be right there with her.

The guy—Fergus, that's what he'd said his name was —rubbed his hand over his face. I couldn't tell whether my punch of reassuring emotion had worn off or if his reaction to his uncovered memories was so intense it overwhelmed any comfort I'd given him before.

"What happened with Nolan?" Lily asked in her softly husky voice. Her gentle tone sent another quiver through me right to my groin. She was powerful, yeah, but she could be so sweet as well. The perfect package.

"I—I don't understand." Fergus gulped audibly. "How could all that—I had no idea—"

Kai leaned closer, peering at the dude like he was scientific specimen. "He worked some kind of power on you to block out those memories—it sounds like for good reason. I'm assuming he didn't hide anything pleasant."

"No. No." Another shudder rippled through the guy's body. His mouth clamped tight. He remembered, but he didn't want to talk about it.

Kai could have used his supernatural skills to make the guy move any way he wanted, but we'd already seen that he couldn't force someone to answer questions that way. His usual methods, working them over with manipulation and persuasion, could take a while. And I wasn't sure they'd work at all on a guy this shaken who'd been terrified of *us* just a few minutes ago.

But I could help with that.

I leaned in and gave Fergus a light but purposeful cuff to the side of his head, drawing on all my affection for and trust in Lily and the guys around me as I did. Urging the sense that he could open up to us, that we'd protect and avenge him as much as he needed, through his skull.

The guy's head swayed to the side, and Lily shot a worried look at me, so maybe I tapped him a tad harder than I'd meant to. It was still tricky judging the exact responses of this new body when I hadn't had any physical form at all for more than twenty years. But Fergus's stance relaxed a little at the same time, a hopeful light coming into his eyes.

"You won't let him come near me again?" he said. "You won't let him use me?"

Lily patted his arm a little awkwardly. "We're doing whatever we can to stop him from hurting anyone again."

Fergus's arms tightened where he was hugging his knees. "He didn't exactly hurt me. He just…"

When he trailed off, Nox shifted on his feet with obvious impatience. Before he could demand that the guy get on with his story, Lily aimed a pointed glance at him. She turned back to Fergus. "Why don't you tell us what he did, and then we'll know what we need to stop him from doing again?"

The dude drew in a shaky breath. "It's kind of hazy. I'm not sure how often it happened. I was pretty little. I think… one time was right after my eighth birthday party. The last time I can remember I was maybe ten?"

Lily nodded. From what she'd said, that was around the age her sister had been when she'd caught Nolan with her.

"Some of it was just him sitting with me," Fergus went on. "He'd pat my back or stick his hand right into my hair, and say things I didn't really understand, and this weird feeling would go through me, kind of like getting shocked by static electricity but stretched out longer. I didn't like it, but it was just weird. It was worse when... sometimes he'd start squeezing my legs or touching me under my shirt and put his mouth on my neck, or he'd get me to sit on his lap, and I could tell—"

He paused, looking like he might be about to vomit. His voice came out even rougher afterward. "It was only touching, and he didn't actually— But still. If I tried to get away, he'd hold on to me harder, and he said my parents would be upset that I hadn't 'helped' him. I don't know what to do."

Lily's face had gone hard and fierce. "There's nothing 'only' about any of that. It's horrible. He isn't going to get away with it."

Fergus's gaze had gone distant as he related his memories. Now it snapped to her with sharper focus. "It wasn't just him. Sometimes his wife came with him. Marie. Sometimes she came on her own. They said it was a good thing to share." He winced.

Lily inhaled sharply. "Both of them. Fuck."

So we had two enemies instead of one. It seemed

28

like the Gauntts spent most of their time together. As far as I could see, that wouldn't make anything much harder.

"When did they give you that mark on your arm?" Kai asked.

"Every time before they left—whoever came— they'd squeeze my arm there and there'd be that electric shock feeling again, all in one spot." Fergus touched his arm where the tiny birthmark had vanished. "Somehow things seemed okay after they did that. Like barely anything had happened."

Kai looked at the rest of us. "And the last time they must have shut off his memories of their visits almost completely."

Lily had knit her brow. "Were they sneaking around your parents all that time? How did they manage to get to you so often?"

A faint, humorless laugh spilled out of Fergus. "My parents knew. They always seemed happy to see the Gauntts. Well, I don't know if they knew what Nolan and Marie were doing exactly, but whatever they told my parents, it made them figure it was a good deal. Mom got a promotion somewhere in there, I think... That's why I believed what the Gauntts said about them wanting me to 'help.' It didn't seem like they'd want to help *me*."

Jett scowled and kicked at the grassy ground. "Of course they knew. Can't count on family to protect you."

Suddenly I was picturing Fergus as a kid, sitting in

29

his bedroom listening to the Gauntts walking up the stairs to "visit" him while his parents chattered away downstairs without a single care. While they got what they wanted without letting themselves care what happened to him. An uncomfortable clenching sensation squeezed around my ribs.

I groped for something happier to say. "But you made it through. You're okay now."

"I don't know, man." Fergus dropped his head into his hands. "I can't wrap my head around all of this. What am I supposed to do now?"

"It wasn't just you," Lily told him. "It seems like it happened to a lot of kids, and it's not your fault at all. Your parents should be ashamed of themselves."

It happened to a lot of kids. I looked down at myself, at my arm. Where I'd seen the mark on Ansel's arm in that photo of him from before I'd taken over.

It'd happened to him. To *me*, sort of. Those memories had fled when we'd shut down his body so it'd be ready for my possession, and none of them had remained when I'd leapt inside, but he'd still experienced the same crap.

His parents, his mother who I'd met briefly when we'd gone to his house—they'd gone along with it just like Fergus's had. Let the Gauntts into their home, looked the other way so they could benefit from the money and prestige...

My jaw clenched. I didn't know how to put a cheerful spin on any of that horribleness. It was shit all the way through. And Lily—there were tears shining in her eyes as she straightened up. What her sister must have gone through, with her mom and stepdad's permission…

The storm of emotion swelled inside me, and right at that moment, my phone—Ansel's old phone—rang.

I froze, my mind blanking momentarily in surprise, and then grabbed it. The call display said it was from *Dad*. My fingers squeezed around the phone as I stared at the word.

"Are you going to answer that?" Nox said, knuckling my arm.

The kind of rage I'd only felt before when seeing assholes attack Lily or my friends surged up inside me. *I shouldn't have to answer.* These people had so much to answer for.

I spun around toward the spot where we'd parked our bikes, jabbing the ignore button on the phone's screen. "I've got something to do."

"What?" Lily said. "Where are you going?"

"To talk to Ansel's parents," I said. "Since he can't speak for himself anymore."

As I marched toward my motorcycle, more fury seared through me. It hazed my mind, drowning out every other sensation. I didn't like it, but I could only think of one way to get it out, to get back to the place where everything had seemed okay: by releasing it on the people who deserved it.

The guys hustled after me, abandoning Fergus. "Hold up," Nox said. "You shouldn't go running off—"

"I need to do this," I repeated, cutting him off. He

should have been able to understand. His parents had treated him like crap. But then he'd had his grandmother. At least he'd had her. So maybe he didn't totally see it after all.

I jumped onto the bike and tore out of the parking lot before anyone else could protest. The growl of engines behind me told me I was being pursued, but I didn't care about that.

There was too much awfulness in the world. It'd hurt Fergus and that girl Peyton; it'd hurt Lily so much my heart ached thinking of the look on her face. It'd hurt her sister and who knew how many other people besides. It'd hurt Ansel, even if he was a prick.

And all these parents had stood by and let it happen.

Why the fuck should they get away with that? Why should we let it slide over and over again?

I was barely paying attention to where I was driving, but my body seemed to know the way. I roared up outside the large, bright house where Ansel had used to live, sprang off my bike, and charged to the front door. My stomach gurgled with an inconvenient pang of hunger, but I got those so often these days that I already had supplies at the ready. I shoved a strip of spicy beef jerky into my mouth with one hand as I pounded on the doorbell and then the door itself with the other.

I was just swallowing when the stiff blond woman who'd answered the door before peered out at me. "Ansel?" she said. "We've been trying to reach you. I know you like to have your fun with your friends and all that, but you really need to be accessible to the family every now and—"

"Like you made hi—made *me* accessible to the Gauntts?" I demanded, realizing in mid-sentence that I'd better pretend to be Ansel for the accusation to make any sense. If I started talking like Ansel was some other guy who wasn't standing in front of her, she might pay more attention to evaluating how crazy her supposed son was than evaluating her own awful behavior.

"I—what?" Ansel's mother said, but she paled at the same time, so I knew she was only playing ignorant. "I don't know what on earth you're talking about, dear. If something's upset you, why don't you come in and—"

"You know exactly what I'm talking about," I snarled. I didn't know exactly where all this rage had come from, how there could be so much seemingly out of nowhere, but it was overflowing and I couldn't see any reason to rein it in. "You and my dad were shitty parents, and you're still being shitty—you turned your back on me and let some creepy people use me for their sick games so you could get a leg up somehow or another, and now you're going to pretend like you have no idea why I'm angry?"

I'd thought she'd paled before. Now she went absolutely white. "I—I—" She couldn't seem to get any syllable out other than that one letter.

"You can't even fucking apologize, can you?" I snapped, and shoved her backward into the house. I stormed after her, taking her up on her invitation belatedly and probably not in the way she'd intended.

But as I opened my mouth to berate her some more, she raised her hands and started clawing at her face.

"How could I have let them come in here and treat you that way?" she screeched, her voice vibrating with anger. "I *am* shitty. I'm the worst garbage. Your father is too. We should both be torn apart for what we did."

Somehow she managed to throw a punch at herself that clocked her in the forehead. As she reeled, I stared at her, my own voice drying up.

I'd infected her with my fury at her and Ansel's dad, and now she was raging at herself. She whipped around, slapping herself across the cheek, yanking at her hair, gnashing her teeth in frustration. She even stomped on her own foot with one of her high-heeled pumps. It was so ridiculous that a laugh bubbled out of me.

Once I started laughing, I couldn't stop. The sight of her flailing around struck me as so funny the anger washed out of me, as if I'd passed all of it on to her.

What had there been to get so worked up about anyway? It'd all worked out in the end. I'd told her off, she was getting her punishment—exactly how it should be.

"Ruin?" Lily's soft voice reached me with an equally gentle hand around my arm. I hadn't realized anyone had followed me into the house, but as I settled down from my bout of laughter, I saw she and all three of my friends were standing behind me in the front hall of Ansel's house.

Ansel's mother was busy smashing an expensive-looking vase over her head while ranting about all her deficiencies as a parent. I figured I could leave her to it now. My work was done.

I turned toward the door with a spring in my step. "All right. Let's get out of here."

Lily peered at me. "Are you okay?"

I beamed at her. "Of course. I did what I needed to do. Now we can get on with finding your sister. You can break the spell on her just like you did with Fergus. It'll all work out!"

And if there was still a tiny burn of fury lurking under the blanket of good cheer I'd wrapped around myself again, I didn't need to worry about it right now.

four

Lily

Marisol's number went to voicemail again. I looked down at the screen with the string of texts I'd also tried sending and bit my lip.

I was pretty sure she had her phone. It wasn't in her things here at the apartment. But one way or another, I'd been blocked there too.

Just in case she might have run back to Mom and Wade, I'd tried calling them too, but Mom's confusion had been obvious even through her cagey remarks. She had no more idea where Marisol was than I did.

So, desperate times called for desperate measures.

I turned back to the laptop I'd placed on the dining

room table. It was set to record through the built-in camera, and I frowned at my image on the screen.

"Is this really going to help us find Marisol? So far the people we know who the Gauntts messed with haven't had contact with them in years. It all happened when they were kids."

"We haven't talked to very many victims," Kai pointed out, sitting on the edge of the table with his legs dangling like there wasn't a perfectly good chair right there under his feet. "The more we can find, the more data we can collect. And predators tend to be creatures of habit. It sounds as if he came to that Fergus guy in his own home, but he might have taken others someplace else."

"Someplace where your sister could be now," Ruin said eagerly, picking up the thread.

Nox prowled by behind me. "Exactly. And then we charge in there, get her back, and rip anyone who tries to get in our way to shreds."

I couldn't say I had any issues with that plan, other than the fact that we didn't know where we'd be charging into yet. I dragged in a breath and eyed my image on the screen. "Okay. So we're going to do this viral video thing. Are you sure it should be me on it? A lot of people around here think I'm crazy. And if the Gauntts find out about it—"

Kai made a dismissive sound. "With the filters, we can make sure your face isn't recognizable. But people are more likely to want to watch a hot girl than some random guy. Especially when it comes to removing clothes." He winked at me.

I wrinkled my nose at him, but I could see his point. I stood up, tugging at the sweater I'd put over a fitted tank top.

We wanted to identify who else in Lovell Rise, Mayfield, or anywhere else in the Gauntts' vicinity might have come under their spell, and we couldn't exactly go around asking everyone to take off their shirt so we could inspect their arms for birthmarks. But the magic of social media meant that it was totally acceptable to ask them to take off their shirts on camera and distribute the image to the entire internet.

It didn't totally make sense to me, but then, I was the weirdo crazy girl, so what did I know?

"This feels silly," I said.

Nox paused in his pacing long enough to grin at me. "It is. But from what I've seen, people *love* silly."

"Especially if they think they can prove they're the only ones who can do it without looking silly," Kai said. "Or that they're the silliest of them all. Basically, any excuse to have a competition."

"Hurray for human nature," Jett muttered from over by the sofa, where he was watching this all go down while nursing a can of cola.

"Okay." I rolled my shoulders. "Let me practice a few times."

"Start the camera rolling," Kai said. "You might get a good take during practice—better to capture it than to have to spend hours trying to recreate it."

"Right." I tapped the button on the screen, watching it switch from green to red, and smiled at myself in my best attempt at looking perky. "Hey, everyone! My boyfriend dared me to prove that I can take off my sweater with just one hand. It's harder than it looks. If you think you can manage it, let's see you try —and hashtag it #sweaterchallenge."

I gripped the top of my left sleeve the way we'd worked out after reading numerous online tutorials— the internet giveth as it receiveth—and managed to wrangle the sweater off me with only a little squirming and half of my hair falling into my face. Not quite the graceful execution I was going for, although from the guys' gazes burning into me, they'd been enjoying the view of my cleavage while I flailed.

I pulled the sweater back on and combed my fingers through my hair. "Okay, let's try that again."

"As many times as you like, Siren," Nox said in a voice that practically liquified my panties.

I glowered at him. "This is for finding Marisol, not starting an orgy."

He shrugged with one of his usual cocky smirks. "I think Kai would say there's a lot of benefit in multitasking."

The brainiac himself didn't even bother responding to that. He motioned to me. "Angle your elbow more to the front this time. That should help the sleeve come off more smoothly."

I nodded. "Got it."

It took four more tries before I managed to whip off

the sweater with stripper-like skill, which wasn't a quality I'd ever thought I'd be aspiring to. I gave it a little twirl in the air and smiled coyly at the camera again. "Don't forget! It's sweater challenge time." I held up my fingers in a victory sign for good measure.

"Perfect." Kai leapt off the table to come around to the computer keyboard. He started tapping away, flicking through filters and cropping the video down to the right length.

"Do you even know how to do video editing?" I asked him.

He gave a dismissive huff. "The basics are simple enough to pick up reading a few user guides. We'll send this to a social media guru I've connected with who's eager to get into my good graces after our last conversation. He'll do the final polishing and figure out all the hashtags and algorithms and whatever the hell else makes it virulent."

"I think the word is 'viral,' Mr. Know-It-All," Jett remarked.

Kai waved him off and kept flicking through the options that came with the recording software. Jett strode over and leaned in next to him, setting down his cola on the table.

"It's not just all your behavioral patterning bullshit," he said. "The video's got to *look* good. Catch the eye. Hit the visual senses in an appealing way."

Kai elbowed him. "That's just three ways of saying essentially the same thing."

"Which just goes to show that you don't really

understand art. Here, let me see." Jett tapped on a few keys and managed to adjust the color of the wall behind me. Then he tweaked the contrast. Suddenly my eyes, set against the startlingly smooth skin the filter had blessed me with, stood out even more starkly with an almost come hither expression.

"Um," I said, "I'm not sure that's the vibe I want to give off."

"Sure it is," Jett said. "You want them to want you. To want to *be* you. Isn't that right?" He raised his eyebrows at Kai.

Kai gazed back at him steadily. "Interesting to hear that point coming from you."

Jett looked as if he'd momentarily swallowed his tongue. It wasn't a secret that *he* didn't want me quite the same way the others did—he'd announced it in front of the whole group a couple of weeks ago. It *was* a secret that despite his announcement, we'd ended up getting very close and personal a few nights ago when we'd ended up sharing a bed together… At least, we had until Jett had become all on-edge about it and stalked out of the room like he hadn't been groping me two seconds ago.

We hadn't talked about that incident since then, and it hadn't seemed right to mention it to any of the other guys. But I still didn't know where the hell I stood with him.

That was hardly important right now while Marisol was missing, though. I gestured broadly at both of them. "Figure out something that works. I spent most

41

of the last seven years not even having a Facebook account—I don't have any more idea what makes something infect social media than you do."

Jett and Kai fell into a discussion about the exact shade they should make my sweater, reaching across to jab the keyboard back and forth like the fairies in Disney's *Sleeping Beauty* adjusting Aurora's dress. I stepped aside and ended up right in Ruin's arms, which really wasn't a bad place to be.

I glanced up over my shoulder at his cheerful face, searching for any sign of the anger he'd shown yesterday. He'd seemed calm enough after he'd inflicted his rage on Ansel's mom, but I'd had no idea that Ruin had that kind of hostility in him to begin with, at least not when we weren't being directly attacked. I guessed it could have simply risen up because he was upset that he couldn't do anything to protect me or Marisol from the Gauntts, but it'd felt like something more.

He'd seemed confused when I'd tried to ask him more about his reaction, though, and I didn't want to badger him.

"One step closer to finding her," he said, pressing a kiss to my temple. "It doesn't seem like the Gauntts outright attacked anyone, right? I'm sure she'll be okay."

"They're just using her as leverage," Nox growled with a flash of his eyes. "How these pricks got away with this crap for so long… I guess that's money for you." He shook his head.

"Money and corporate power and influence," I said, and sighed. "I wonder how many kids he's gone after.

Him and Marie too. They probably have others they're going on their 'visits' these days." I shuddered, the warmth of Ruin's body not enough to ward off the chill of that thought. "And all those parents going along with it…"

Kai looked up from where it appeared he and Jett had finally settled on a grudging compromise about the video's color scheme. "The Gauntts could obviously influence Marisol's behavior, presumably through that mark. They quite possibly provoked the bullies against you—at least some of them. Some were probably just following the herd. For all we know, at least a few of the parents were older victims who were affected too."

I hadn't considered that possibility. "But—the Gauntts aren't that much older than most of our parents. They're, what, in their 60s? My mom is forty-eight. Wade is at least fifty. When they were kids, Nolan and Marie wouldn't have been much past their teens. How much social power did they have then to convince *those* kids' parents to let them do their secret business?"

Nox shrugged. "It's all inherited, right? Thrivewell has been around for, like, a century. They had their own parents' influence behind them."

Ruin's head lifted. "Do you think their parents had magic powers too? Is it a family thing? Maybe that's how they got their business to be so big and popular."

Kai nudged his glasses up his nose. "You know, that's not a bad point. We can't be sure what the full extent of their supernatural abilities is, and what we do know about altering people's memories could definitely be useful in some business contexts."

"Fuckers," Nox grumbled, and raised his chin. "Doesn't matter. They could be Superman and Wonder Woman, and we'd still crush them."

The conversation was making me feel depressed rather than optimistic about our chances, regardless of Nox's bravado. I eased away from Ruin and went to join Jett where he'd lingered by the computer, studying the video image. This was the one concrete way I had of trying to take on the Gauntts for now.

"Do you think you've made me pretty enough yet?" I teased.

Jett glanced over at me, and I was abruptly aware that I'd stopped close enough that he'd only have needed to lean over a few inches for his shoulder to brush mine. He paused for a beat too long, our gazes locked together.

"You're always pretty," he said abruptly. Then he yanked his eyes away, followed by the rest of his body as he retreated from the computer. "*I* think it's good to go."

Nox strolled over, giving Jett an assessing look I couldn't quite read before contemplating the screen himself. "Well, you two seem to know what you're doing. Send it off to whoever's going to do the final spiffing up and let's get on to the part where we find out whose heads we need to crack."

At those words, I paused, thinking of the other quest the Skullbreakers had been on before Marisol's disappearance. They'd finally found out which rival gang had been responsible for murdering them all those years ago.

"It's going to take at least a day or two for the video to catch on, if it even does," I said. "Don't you need to go after the Skeleton Corps too?"

Nox folded his arms over his chest. "I've told you before, and I'll keep telling you—you're our first priority. That includes your sister."

"Yeah, but—if we can't do anything for her right now anyway— And it'll be hard for you to help me if they come after you all over again." I tipped my head toward the window. "If you track them down and crack some of *their* heads, maybe some of their people will have heard something about Marisol too. They are supposed to be the most connected gang in the city, right?"

Nox stewed on that for a few moments before a grin stretched across his face. "If you're that eager to get started on the beatdowns, who am I to say no? And we do need to pay back our murderers in kind—with twenty-one years' interest on top of that."

five

Lily

I wasn't sure I'd ever get totally used to riding on the back of a motorcycle. It was thrilling and terrifying all at once, even with the bulky helmet fixed on my head to theoretically prevent *my* skull from getting broken. The Skullbreakers weren't interested in inflicting their brand of havoc on their own.

Small mercies.

Nox had insisted that I ride with him, of course, even though there was less room behind his massive frame than any of the other guys'. But that just meant I had to tuck myself that much closer to him, breathing in the smell of his leather jacket and the musk that was all his own underneath, unable to stop myself from remembering the times I'd had him between my thighs in other ways.

Being around these guys was turning me into a nympho as well as a psycho. But at least I was a well-satisfied nympho.

The four bikes roared through the streets and slammed to a halt outside a dingy-looking mechanic shop. The Skullbreakers all hopped off, Nox gripping my elbow to help me as I slid from the seat. He gave me a brief glance with a tensing of his jaw and a flash of protective concern in his eyes.

One of the hodgepodge of low-level criminal allies the guys had scrounged up in the past few days had given us a tip about where a few men they knew to be part of the Skeleton Corps were working today. We were here to confront them. I suspected Nox would rather I was about a hundred miles away from anything to do with the gang who'd killed him and the others twenty-one years ago, but he also knew there was no way in hell I was hiding anymore.

I was part of the Skullbreakers now. He'd acknowledged it, and so he had to live with it. I'd even helped them out with their past head-cracking and info-searching.

He didn't tell me to stay behind, just marched onward a couple of steps in front of me. Kai came up beside him, and Jett and Ruin formed a shield on either side of me. I was with them, but no one could get at me without going through them first.

I was pretty okay with that.

The hum of my magic tickled through my chest alongside my nerves. Nox tested the front door of the shop's office, found it locked, and proceeded to kick it in with a ram of his heel. The lock snapped, and we all marched inside.

By the time we'd crossed the small office to the expansive mechanic bay it led into, three guys had leapt to their feet among the cars. It looked like they'd been working on a couple of them: a sleek red Jaguar and a posh silver BMW. I'd be willing to bet my entire life savings, as meager as they were, that they weren't fixing up these cars so much as fixing to sell them to the highest bidder after they removed all signs of the legitimate owners they'd stolen them from.

"What the fuck are you doing?" one of the Skeleton Corps guys demanded, smacking a wrench against his open palm.

"We popped by for a little chat," Nox said in a sarcastic tone, but his gaze had veered to the Jag. He stepped closer to skim his fingers over the edge of the roof. "This is a nice find here. How much do you sell these for?"

Kai let out a cough. "*Nox.*"

The Skullbreakers leader jerked his attention back to the more important matter at hand. I made a mental note of his car preferences in case I was ever in a position to pick one up—you know, as a Christmas present or something.

"You're with the Skeleton Corps?" he growled, fixing his eyes on each of the guys in turn.

The guy with the wrench narrowed his eyes. "You're those dickhead punks who've been rampaging all over town. Haven't you gotten the message yet? There's no place for you here, and no one cares about your *feelings* about some pricks who died a gazillion years ago."

"Twenty-one," Kai corrected, like he couldn't help being pedantic, which maybe he couldn't.

Jett pushed forward to flank Nox at his other side. "It seems like *you're* the ones who haven't gotten the message."

Ruin chuckled, waving his fists. "And you'd better be worried about your own feelings, because it's not going to feel *good* when we've stomped you into little pieces."

The Corps guy didn't even bother to reply. He made some gesture I barely caught, and the three guys launched themselves at us like one being.

They should have had the advantage. There were only three of them, but they were armed—the one guy with his very large wrench and the other two with guns they whipped out as they came at us. The Skullbreakers had shown up apparently empty-handed, although I knew they had their own pistols tucked away in easy reach. The thing was, these jerks clearly hadn't gotten the news about just how much my men could do with their empty hands.

Nox swung his fists in quick succession, the burst of energy that shot from them extending his reach. He smacked the gun from one guy's grasp and then clocked him in the jaw hard enough to send him reeling into a backflip that would have impressed most Olympic judges before he was even close enough for Nox to touch.

Kai ducked and jabbed the other gunman in the stomach, ordering, "Stop your colleagues from attacking us," as he did.

That guy jerked around toward the wrench-man like he was a puppet on strings, but before he had to tackle the wrench, Jett and Ruin double-teamed the guy. Jett, his supernatural talent for altering appearances not being particularly helpful in a fight, simply kicked the guy's legs out from under him, sending him staggering right into Ruin's fist. His mouth stretched into a fierce grin, Ruin smacked the guy's hand up to sock him with his own wrench for good measure.

The rhythm of the smacks, thuds, and groans filled my ears, and it occurred to me with a distant sort of uneasiness that I wasn't particularly shocked or horrified by any of the violence anymore. These were my men, dealing out justice the way they knew how, and I was okay with that too. There was almost a music in the sounds of the fighting—an urgent, gritty sort of melody. It resonated through me.

A twinge came into my throat. I could have put words to it, could have sung out a vehement chorus to match our determination to see our mission through, but the impulse dwindled as quickly as it'd risen up. The ache of grief swallowed it up.

How could I sing when I'd lost Marisol, in even direr circumstances than before?

Ruin's victim stumbled backward. I found out what emotion our ever-cheerful guy had inflicted on the leader of this crew when he dropped to his knees in front of us and kowtowed his head to the cement floor. "Have mercy. We're not worthy."

Ruin cackled gleefully and spun toward the first guy, who'd caught his balance against the Jaguar. His gaze shot to his gun, lying on the floor several feet across the bay, but the second he moved, his own friend was on him. The guy Kai had punched tackled the other Skeleton Corps member, and they both tumbled to the floor.

Kai stalked over and gave the guy on the floor a kick to the ribs. "Lie still and don't make a sound."

The guy immediately stiffened, his lips pressing tightly shut, but it turned out that at least today, Kai couldn't impose his will on more than one person at a time. The man who'd tackled his friend leapt up and lunged at Kai.

Nox lashed out with his foot. Even though he was five feet away, his powers neatly tripped the attacker. The guy fell flat on his face, and Jett knocked both him and the other guy unconscious with a couple of quick blows. Ruin bounded over and tossed one of the now-limp guys on top of the other. He sat on them both. "Everything secure here!" he announced.

Kai stayed where he was, looking ready to aim another commanding strike if need be. Jett prowled through the bay to confirm no one was hiding amid the equipment. Nox loomed over the guy who was still bobbing his head up and down over the floor like one of those drinking-bird toys.

"Oh, please," the guy mumbled. "Take pity on me. I would never have talked back if I'd realized how great you are."

Nox smirked at Ruin. "I like the tune you got this guy playing. Let's use that one again sometime." He turned back to the pleading man. "You deserve to be crushed into dirt, but we'll make an exception if you prove how sorry you are."

"Of course! Anything. Just say the word."

Nox set his hands on his hips. "Tell us who's in charge of the Skeleton Corps, and where we can find them."

The man looked up at him, his face falling in apparent regret. "I can't tell you that. I don't know."

Nox bared his teeth and leaned down with his fist poised. "Do I need to give you even more motivation?"

"No, no, please, I really don't! You have to understand—no one at our level knows. The Corps operates in squads. We only know who's in our squad and one guy higher up who we answer to. But the guy who gives us our marching orders isn't the head honcho."

"Would *he* know who's in charge?" Kai asked.

The guy made a face. "I'm not sure. He might have his own squad leader who isn't the top boss either. I have no idea how many levels there are. We're at the bottom."

"Well, it's a place to start." Nox crouched in front of

him, cracking his knuckles. "Where do we find the man you answer to?"

"I—I don't know where he'd be right now. But we meet him once a week around the back of the convenience store at River and Princeton."

Nox made a skeptical sound. "How about you show us this convenience store, just so we can make sure you're not sending us on a wild goose chase?"

The guy scrambled to his feet like he'd been offered a trip to the Bahamas instead of ordered to betray his overlords. He gestured for us to follow him and hustled out of the mechanic shop.

"Keep a close eye on him," Kai muttered to the others under his breath as we left behind the two Skeleton Corps guys who were just starting to come to. "We don't know how long Ruin's emotional voodoo will last."

It turned out the convenience store in question was only a five-minute walk away, and the guy remained his newly deferential self the entire walk over. He swept his arm toward the building like he was presenting us with a prize and then walked around back to show us the alley, planting his feet in the exact spot where he said he normally stood when he met this mid-level boss, whose name he didn't even know.

"We're due to meet with him again next Monday," he said. "Seven sharp."

"At night, I assume," Kai said dryly, and the guy nodded vigorously.

"Listen," Nox said. "You're going to make an excuse

to your buddies to keep them from showing up on time so that we can have a word with the dude first. And you're not going to let it slip to anyone that you gave this away. Understood?"

The guy nodded again, his eyes wide, but apprehension twisted my stomach.

"Can we be sure he'll keep to that?" I asked. "Ruin's influence is going to wear off way before then."

Jett cocked his head and stepped in. He looked the guy straight in the eyes from just a foot away and slammed his hand against the guy's chest. "I'll give him something to remember us by. So that he keeps in mind just how hard we can come down on him and how easily we can mess him up if he doesn't do what we say."

He jerked down the collar of the man's shirt to show the blood-red handprint he'd imprinted on the guy's skin like a tattoo. A shudder ran down the man's back. Jett's talents might not be super useful in a battle, but they did have one advantage over the other guys': his were permanent. My apartment walls hadn't lost the color he'd given them days ago.

"I'll remember," the guy said, shaking.

"You'd better," Nox growled. "Because Jett's right. If we hear that you tattled, you'd better believe we can track you down and make you pay in all kinds of ways. You saw how we handled you and your bros back at the shop. We can make you do whatever we want to each other… and to yourself. You'd *kill* yourself if we told you to."

The guy nodded again with a jerk of his head, and his hand shot up to rub at the opposite arm.

Something in me went deathly still. "What are you scratching?" I demanded abruptly.

The guy's gaze darted to me. "I—I just had an itch—"

"Show us your arm," I said, my heart beating faster. A ghost of an itch—the itch that'd niggled at me every so often for years until I'd defeated it—rose up under my own skin.

The guy warily shrugged off his jean jacket and peeled up his sleeve. Just a few inches below his armpit, a small, roundish pink birthmark showed against his tan skin.

I swallowed hard. "The Gauntts messed with him too."

Kai frowned. "We knew they got around."

The guy stared at us. "The Gauntts? You mean the Thrivewell people? I don't have anything to do with them. I mean, I remember they came around for some kind of project that was something to do with school back when I was a kid, but—what are you talking about?"

I glanced at Kai. "Make sure he'll cooperate?"

Kai understood what I meant without any further instruction. He socked the guy in the shoulder. "Stand still while Lily gives you your memories back."

I stepped up to the guy and grasped his arm. He gaped at me even as he followed Kai's command. "I don't get it."

Even though he was one of the enemy, even though he might have been one of the dipshits who'd defaced my apartment and tried to stop me from claiming it, a twinge of sympathy ran through my chest. "You will," I said. "But it isn't going to be fun. I'm sorry."

Then I focused on the mark on his arm, bringing the hum of energy inside me roaring up to the surface.

six

Nox

"Did they mess up half the kids in the county?" I growled as we strode back to our bikes. The Skeleton Corps doofus hadn't told us much about his experiences with the Gauntts, but the horror that'd come over his face and the way he'd cringed from talking about it was a story all on its own. He'd mumbled something about "parading around" and "Why would they want my clothes off?" which was enough to draw a very sick picture.

"They obviously didn't discriminate between rich kids and families from the wrong side of the tracks," Kai remarked in his matter-of-fact way. Usually I liked that

57

he didn't get worked up about much of anything. Right now, it kind of made me want to punch him.

"Hurray for equal opportunity," Lily grumbled. Her face was even paler than usual, her expression pained. That made me want to punch several people. Preferably starting with Nolan and Marie Gauntt.

But even as my hands tightened into fists, I knew that barging to the Thrivewell building and starting a fist fight wasn't going to fix this problem. For starters, I wasn't quite so cocky that I figured I could make it up twenty floors of that building including the private elevator Kai and Lily had described without security catching me. I was a force to be reckoned with and even more powerful with my new ghostly energies, but I wasn't invincible, and pretending I was would only hurt the woman and the guys who were counting on me in the long run.

"What are we going to do?" Ruin asked, his voice taut with both eagerness and tension. We'd seen how pissed off the whole situation made him already. I'd never pried much about what his childhood had been like, but I suspected it hadn't been as sunshine-and-rose-y as his current attitude. He bobbed on his feet with his strides like he couldn't wait to launch himself in whatever direction I pointed him in.

The problem was, I wasn't totally sure what direction that should be. I was the leader of the Skullbreakers—it was my job to get us on the right course and see us through this shitfest. But we had a whole banquet of trouble on our plates, and it was hard to tell what we should dig into first that wouldn't make the rest come crashing down on our heads.

Life had definitely been simpler before I'd died.

That thought brought back the pang of loss and anger from when I'd discovered who else had died while I'd been lingering in limbo. The one guiding light I'd had in my own childhood, who'd maybe saved me from the kind of fate the Gauntts' victims had met. My actual parents probably would have sold me for coke or another round at the slots if they'd been ambitious enough to try.

I couldn't talk to Gram the usual way anymore, but maybe she'd have some insights for me anyway. Hell, it was possible her spirit had stuck around like ours had and just had been off running errands or something the last time I'd stopped by her grave.

"I need to think," I announced as we reached the bikes. "Figure out the big picture and how we rearrange it."

"I vote for starting by bashing in the Gauntts' faces," Jett put in.

"We'll get there." I dragged in a breath, not liking to let Lily out of my sight but knowing she'd be in good hands. "The rest of you take Lily back to the apartment. Hash out what we've learned if you want and see what brilliant ideas you all come up with. I have to take care of a couple of things while I mull this over."

The guys looked reluctant, but they didn't question me. Lily didn't have quite the same respect for my authority, but then, I wouldn't have wanted her to feel she had to shut up and fall in line.

She touched my arm, studying my face. "Are you okay? You're not going to go on some kamikaze mission on your own or something crazy like that, are you?"

I had to grin at her. I didn't think it'd ever stop feeling good having this woman concerned about me. Knowing I'd earned that much affection. "Well, now that you've suggested it…" When she grimaced, I leaned in and gave her a swift but firm kiss. "I'm not planning on going anywhere near our enemies at the moment, Minnow," I assured her. "If they come at me, they'll be sorry. But when we take them down, you're going to be right there with me."

"Good," she said, giving my arm a squeeze and stealing another kiss before she let me go.

I mounted my bike and tore off in the opposite direction from the others. Before I went to pay my respects, I stopped at a couple of stores to procure appropriate offerings. Gram had always believed in bringing hostess gifts, and she expected me to mind my manners at least while I was within her sights.

Unless someone else in her sights was being a total jackass. Then I had free rein to throw politeness out the window. Gram hadn't been any pushover.

The cemetery where she was buried was looking pretty quiet. I parked my motorcycle off by itself and tramped across the grassy slopes between the shiny new stones toward the small plot that was Gram's.

She hadn't had much to her name, but she had

insisted on buying the plot well before we'd thought there was any chance of her kicking the bucket. Maybe she'd paid for the headstone in advance too. *I don't want you having to worry about what to do with my decrepit bones when I leave this world,* she'd told me more than once. *It's not like I'll be around to care about any fancy to-dos anyway.* Although maybe she'd been wrong about that last part.

She definitely hadn't gone for anything fancy. Her stone stood out amid the others in its row for just how humble it was. Amid the polished marble and towering granite stood a stumpy chunk of rough limestone, no filigree or hopeful symbols chiseled into it, just her name—*Gloria Louise Savage*—and her dates.

Eighty-three years—not too bad a run. Somehow I'd never realized she was quite as old as she was when I'd been living with her. She must have been in her fifties when she'd taken me in at age seven and her sixties by the time I was in my teens, but she'd had so much energy and attitude I'd never thought of her as a senior citizen.

I stood across from the headstone and brought out my offerings. First came the bottle of strawberry iced tea. If you asked me, the stuff was foul, but Gram had guzzled it like it was the elixir of life. She hadn't drunk much else.

I unscrewed the cap and poured it liberally over the grass. Maybe a little would soak into those old bones of hers and give her one last sip.

Then I placed a copy of the latest bizarro tabloid

against her stone, because Gram enjoyed nothing more than finding out who'd recently been kidnapped by snake aliens from outer space or communed with Bigfoot in the Alps. Next to it, I set a snazzy gauze scarf that was all neon pink-and-orange flowers.

Gram used to have a scarf for every type of weather. *No one wants to see this chicken neck of mine*, she'd say. Well, now she could be fashionably insecure in the afterlife too.

No sense of a supernatural presence had touched my awareness while I'd been standing there. Now that I was back in a body, I wasn't sure if I'd be more in tune with a loitering ghost than Lily had been with us pre-possession. Was it possible Gram *was* here, and I just couldn't tell?

That idea was even more awful than her being totally gone, so I'd assume that she was either resting in peace or conducting a very busy spectral social life. Maybe there were ghostly book clubs and craft fairs and who knew what else that no one had bothered to invite me and my crew to.

"Hey, Gram," I said anyway, in case she was looking down on me from some better place, the way people talked about. "I brought you a few things I figure they might not have in large supply Upstairs... or Downstairs, if you decided to chill with the Devil. I wouldn't blame you. I'm sure he's a lot more fun."

The breeze rustled through the nearby trees, but no voice carried on it. No hint of a hug brushed across my shoulders. But I found that I wanted to keep talking. I could see her in my mind's eye, standing over a much younger me while I sat on the hardest of the kitchen chairs, her hands on her hips, asking me what ridiculousness I'd gotten myself into now and whether the other people'd had it coming.

"I'm sorry I didn't make it back in time to see you off," I said. "I hope you had a little company, and that maybe you suspected I wasn't really all gone. You were always pretty sharp like that. Figured out stuff before I even knew. Gave me a lot of practice at keeping the stuff I shouldn't be doing on the down low, which has definitely been useful. So, thank you for that."

I shifted on my feet, rocking back on my heels in silence as a couple walked by on a nearby path. What I said to Gram wasn't any of their business, especially if it might incriminate me in a court of law. I waited until they were way off by a statue of some angel who looked constipated before I spoke up again.

"You always told me I could own the whole world if I was willing to take it on. I'm pretty sure you were exaggerating and just trying to be inspirational, but it kind of feels like I do have to take on the whole world right now. We're going after some big guns, bigger than I ever thought I'd be tangling with, and that's meaning I have to go big too. But it's getting fucking crazy. Like, really crazy, not just what Lily would call crazy. You never got to meet her, but I think the two of you would get along pretty well."

I paused, rummaging through my thoughts. The Gram in my head said, *How crazy are we talking about here?* like I'd imagine she would have if she'd really been here. So naturally, I answered.

"Well, we've all got superpowers. We're whooping people's asses without even touching them, jumbling up their emotions and using mind control and—we'd probably end up in one of your tabloids with the aliens and the Bigfoots. So that's pretty crazy. And we're fighting against one of the biggest corporations in the country, maybe the world, at the same time. But all that is fine. We've got the tools we need to bring the bastards down."

What's the problem then?

I let out a grunt of frustration. "I'm just thinking about all the stuff we're going to have to do to go after them, and it's so much more than I ever figured on when we were just stomping around Lovell Rise… What if I go too far? What if I bite off too much all at once, and the guys and Lily end up choking too? I *want* to tear apart this whole fucking city right now, but if you think about it, that's a hell of a lot of rubble coming down on our heads."

So dodge it, Gram said. *You're fast on your feet still, aren't you? If you're up against big, then you have to go big or go home. If you're up against crazy, sanity's overrated. Hit them where it hurts and don't give them a chance to hit you back, or you might as well not start the fight at all.*

Even though those words were only scraps of things she'd said before, stitched into a sort of patchwork in my imagination, a weird sense of comfort settled over me. Because it wasn't hard at all to picture her actually saying that. And like in most things, she'd have been right.

We had to take on the Gauntts and the Skeleton Corps. There wasn't any "if" about it. And if we were going to smash those fuckers to smithereens, it was going to take everything we had in us, no matter how insane.

I'd had a wild fury bubbling inside me from the moment the bullet one of the Skeleton Corps pricks had fired shattered my skull. Any qualms I'd still had left at that point in my life had gone out the window with my brains.

That wasn't a defect. That was a gift. I could be as fucking savage as I wanted to be without giving a shit what anyone else would think about it.

There was no way the Corps or the Gauntts could be prepared for what I was willing to unleash on them. It was time to lean in and step up.

SEVEN

Lily

I'd thought that I was ready for this new phase in our fight with the Gauntts. But looking up over the stone wall at the posh house—mansion, let's be real—in the Mayfield suburbs, all I wanted to do was make like a gopher and burrow away into the ground.

"Are you sure this is a good idea?" I asked.

Beside me, Nox snorted. "Good isn't a metric we're using these days. It's the right idea if we're going to get a grip on all the shit these pricks are up to. Come on."

He held out his hands to boost me up like he already had the three other guys. I planted my feet on his palms, gripped his broad shoulders for balance, and swiveled to grasp the top of the wall as he lifted me. With a not-particularly-graceful amount of squirming, I swung my legs over the top and dropped down on the other side.

Nox gave a couple of hops and managed between his substantial height and the punch of energy he could produce from his limbs to vault himself high enough to clamber over the wall on his own. The four of us clustered together at the edge of the lawn, partly hidden by a cherry tree, eyeing the big beige-and-blue mansion where the Gauntts lived.

All of them. It turned out that Nolan and Marie lived with the younger generation, Thomas and Olivia. I wasn't even sure which of the second generation was Nolan and Marie's kid and which had married into the family. The house looked big enough to hold about ten different families, so I guessed it wasn't particularly crowded that way, even if staying under the parents' roof was kind of odd these days.

Maybe they just sat around and planned all the next moves of their business over dinner and drinks.

Did the younger Gauntts have special powers too? Were they in on the whole exploit-the-children project Nolan and Marie had going on? None of the victims we'd talked to had mentioned anyone else, but as far as I knew, Thomas and Olivia were in their thirties. They could have been practically kids themselves when Ansel and Peyton and the others had been roped in.

They might be victims too.

A shiver passed through me at the thought. Kai's keen eyes caught the reaction, but he read the wrong reason into it.

"There's definitely no one home," he said. "I confirmed that all four of them left for that business conference before I left the office. And we've had a couple of the sharper new recruits keeping a careful eye on the place all day. No one's driven in."

"They could have housekeeping staff who live on site," Jett pointed out.

Nox hummed in agreement. "They'd practically need an army to keep that place all clean and orderly."

"They must want their privacy too, though," I said. "They get up to a lot of crazy things… They wouldn't want some maid stumbling on them working magic or talking about how great the last molestation went and spreading the word around."

Kai nodded. "There've been no rumors about the Gauntts that've gotten enough traction to warrant even a news article. I've combed the archives of the internet thoroughly." He grimaced, and I remembered his past complaints about wading through the chaos of the world wide web. "I actually identified a woman who does cleaning for them and chatted her up yesterday. She only comes by twice a week—not including today —and she commented that the house is kind of spooky with no one there."

Ruin shuffled his feet, his eyes bright with anticipation. "Let's get on with it, then! Maybe we'll find Lily's sister in there."

I wished I could feel as hopeful as he sounded. "I don't think they'd stash kidnapping victims in their own home. But they might have left some kind of clue about where they *are* holding her."

We pulled up the hoods of the hoodies we'd all donned, extra big so the fabric would shadow our faces. Then we set off across the lawn with our heads low, checking carefully for any signs of life or electronic surveillance. The Gauntts might not have any human beings watching over the property, but it was hard to believe they wouldn't have some kind of security cameras.

"What about the alarm system?" I asked as we approached the house. There was about a snowball's chance in hell they didn't have one of those too.

"Not a problem," Kai said with his usual cool confidence, and waggled his fingers. "We still have electricity on our side. So sad that there'll be a blackout in the neighborhood right when five disreputable types were scoping out the place." He glanced at me and gave me one of his narrow smiles. "Well, four disreputable types and one totally admirable woman who's somehow gotten suckered in by them."

I snorted. "You're doing all this to help me find my sister. Seems like if anyone got suckered, it's you."

"Oh, we're more than adequately compensated," Nox teased, slinging an arm around me and pinching my butt. When I glowered at him, he chuckled and let me go. "That blackout's going to take all of us. Ready?"

The four guys walked right up to the house where the electrical service connected to the building. They raised their hands and without speaking seemed to agree on their timing. Leaping forward, they smacked the wall simultaneously.

A crackling sound burst through the air, followed by a furious sizzling. Then there was a faint *pop* like a cork coming out of a bottle of champagne.

Even late in the afternoon, it wasn't dark enough yet for there to be any lights in view that I could watch blinking off. But the guys seemed totally confident it'd worked. Nox marched up to the front door and slapped his hand against the electronic keypad next. There was another crackle, and the deadbolt in the door slid over. He turned the knob, and we all waltzed inside like we owned the place.

Kai checked the hall light switch and confirmed that it wasn't working. We peered through the shadows at the grand entryway that led to a sweeping mahogany staircase.

Jett let out a low whistle. "It's fucking absurd, but when it comes to absurd levels of pomposity, they do know how to decorate a place."

We treaded farther in over thick, discreetly patterned rugs, past framed landscape paintings and side tables with elegant vases, under unlit brass light fixtures dangling from ornate moldings. There definitely was an eerie hush to the place—I could see why the maid might find it unnerving. But presumably they paid her well enough that she'd gotten over it. It must have taken her the entire day to clean all these rooms.

The Gauntts didn't just keep their home posh. It was also painstakingly neat. I guessed that probably wasn't too difficult to accomplish when they spent most of their lives at work—compared to, say, living in an apartment with four guys who had bottomless pits for stomachs and the frequent urge to test out their budding supernatural powers on everything in their vicinity.

We looked through all the cupboards and drawers in the painfully white kitchen and turned up nothing but standard utensils and dishes, like something out of a home showroom. Several plain round magnets dappled the immense stainless-steel fridge, but none of them actually stuck anything to the surface. No notes, no photos, no delivery menus.

It barely felt like anyone lived here at all.

Wandering through what they might have called living or sitting or family rooms—there were so many of them I had no idea which was which—we found a few signs of life. Someone had left a novel—Stephen King, not the kind of high-brow stuff I'd have expected —on an ebony coffee table. A partly filled out pad of sudoku puzzles lay in an end table's drawer next to a precisely sharpened pencil. I didn't think we could report them to the police on the basis of banal pastimes, though.

The TV room threw me for a bit of a loop. I found myself staring at the rows of movies stashed away behind glossy glass cabinet doors on one side of the huge flatscreen TV. They had an entire set of Disney animated flicks and most of Pixar's oeuvre too, alongside war films and historical dramas and a sizeable collection of horror that fit with the Stephen King book.

Ruin came up beside me and cocked his head. "Young at heart?" he suggested, but even he couldn't quite sell the joke.

Did they bring their victims here sometimes and put on the movies to distract them? Or did the Gauntts just have an unusual appreciation for family features?

It turned out the answer was something else entirely —something I wouldn't have predicted in a million years after seeing the rest of the house. We headed upstairs, stepped into the first bedroom off the broad hallway, and realized they didn't need to bring kids here to visit.

They had kids living right here with them.

The bedroom was painted bright yellow with the furniture done up in a palate of primary colors that made Jett wince. If we'd had any doubt about it being for one specific kid and not occasional visitors, a framed photo on the dresser showed the four Gauntts we'd known about as well as a boy and a girl who looked to be seven or eight, nestled between Thomas and Olivia's arms.

I strode out of that room and into the next one, which looked a lot like the first but all done up in pinks and lilacs. The girl's bedroom, obviously, unless the Gauntts had decided to completely reverse traditional gender expression.

"How did we not know Thomas and Olivia had kids?" I demanded.

Kai was frowning as he poked around the bedroom, which was as painfully neat as the rest of the place. It was hard to believe children actually inhabited this space and not, say, kid-shaped robots. Which would have been an interesting development, but the Gauntts had given every sign of being supernaturally inclined, not mechanical geniuses.

"I don't know," he said. "I haven't seen anything about them in their schedules or heard anyone mention them. The kids must have joined them on this trip or else be staying with other relatives."

Ruin looked unusually downcast. "Who looks after them while their parents are working all the time?"

"They could have a nanny who just doesn't live in the house—she only comes when the kids are out of school and the parents at work," I said, more to reassure Ruin than to justify anything the Gauntts did. I didn't like seeing his good cheer diminish, and they seemed to be having that effect on him a lot these days.

"Or maybe they use their supernatural voodoo on the kids too, so they'll be obedient little dupes," Nox growled. "It'd explain how fucking tidy this place is even with them running around."

It would. And it could be that the Gauntts did other things to those kids, just like they did to those outside their family. I hugged myself, my stomach turning.

Jett had stalked back into the boys' room. I followed him and found him studying the photograph.

"I don't think they're genetically related," he said abruptly. "Their features are too different."

Kai joined us and took the photo from him. He made a thoughtful sound. "I see what you mean. Good eye—of course, that makes sense, coming from you. You know…" His forehead furrowed as he examined the picture even more intently. "I can't tell which of the second generation is related to Nolan and Marie. They both look too different as well."

"There are things like recessive genes and whatever, right?" I said. "Unusual features popping up?"

"Not usually to this extent. The bone structure… set of the eyes… Hmm." Kai snapped a picture of the photo with his phone, presumably to ruminate over more later.

"They might have taken Marisol someplace that their own kids go to, right?" Ruin said, bringing back the optimism.

"Maybe," I agreed. "See if you can find anything about lessons they take or even what school they go to."

We searched through both of the kids' bedrooms and turned up nothing but clothes, books, and evidence that they were at least allowed electronic devices, as there was a charging cable plugged in next to one of the beds. Nothing even indicated what the kids' names were. I stepped back into the hall, my skin creeping.

"I don't like this," I said to Nox. "Everything about these people just seems to get worse and worse. How can we protect their *own* kids from them?"

He rubbed his hand up and down my back. "Rescuing your sister comes first. Then we'll worry about the rest. Hell, if we blow up all the adult Gauntts, someone else will have to adopt the kids."

I raised my eyebrows at him. "Is that the plan now? We're looking to turn them into human dynamite?"

He shrugged with a sly gleam in his dark eyes. "After seeing this place, I don't think I'd trust a simple bullet to do the trick."

He might have had a point there.

Ruin's voice traveled from one of the rooms farther down the hall. "Huh, this is pretty funny."

We all hustled over to join him. He was standing in a bedroom clearly used by adults, with a classy sleigh bed and matching furnishings in dark wood. On the vanity, next to a jewelry box, stood a vase full of dried bullrushes.

Ruin was leaning close. He gave an audible sniff and glanced at the rest of us. "I swear they're from our marsh too!"

Kai gave him a skeptical look. "I'd imagine all marsh vegetation smells pretty similar," he said.

Nox bent in to take a whiff. "I don't know," he said. "We were steeping in that stuff for more than two decades. It does smell awfully familiar."

"What other marshes are around here anyway?" Jett pointed out.

Kai huffed. "They probably bought it from the Pottery Barn or someplace because they thought it was pretty."

"I don't think that's the weird part," I said, and

motioned to a portrait hanging on the wall on the other side of the room.

The oil painting showed a couple who appeared to be middle-aged, but they didn't look like Nolan and Marie or the photos I'd seen of Thomas and Olivia. The man had a bulbous nose that would have been unmistakable if I'd seen it on anyone else, and the woman had a bit of a cleft chin.

"Who the heck are *they*?" I asked. "And why do the Gauntts have their portrait hanging in their bedroom?"

"Distant ancestors?" Nox suggested.

"Their clothes aren't that old-fashioned," Kai said. "I'd say those are '40s era. 1940s, that is, not 1840s or something."

"I guess they could be grandparents or great-grandparents," I said, but that explanation didn't sit totally right. Maybe it was just the way the painted figures' eyes seemed to follow me when I walked back out of the room. "There's nothing around that tells us anything about what they've done with Marisol."

"We have a few new leads I can follow up on," Kai said, but optimism didn't sound as natural on him as it did coming from Ruin.

Who was now in another bedroom, calling us over. "We know they really love marshes!"

I stepped in after him and saw what he meant. This was clearly the main master bedroom, presumably where Nolan and Marie slept. There was a faint, crisp scent of cologne lingering in the air that made me think of the imposing man who'd laughed at my magical display. But what drew my attention were the vases on either side of the sprawling California king bed.

They didn't fit with the rest of the décor at all, really. They were too untidy, too wild. Both of them were stuffed full of reeds and bullrushes that did look as if they'd been plucked right out of the marsh where I'd nearly drowned fourteen years ago.

eight

Kai

I leaned against the counter in the school office and formed my best ingratiating smile. "I really am very sorry to bother you about this issue. It's just so important that I make sure I have the correct information so that we don't miss any potential risk factors that could compromise the children's health."

Between the posh formality I'd taken on to fit with the private school atmosphere and my appeal to health concerns, I had the secretary wrapped around my finger. It'd only taken me a matter of seconds after I walked in the door to notice the little signs of hypochondria: the hands slightly chafed from over-washing, the not one but three bottles of hand sanitizer all within easy reach in different directions across her desk area, the faint whiff of tea tree oil that hung around her. It must be awfully hard keeping herself so germ-free while surrounded by elementary school kids.

"Of course, of course," she said with a nervous giggle, and tapped away at her keyboard. The keys were so brightly white I wondered if she bleached them daily. She knit her brow at the screen. "Nolan and Marie Gauntt, you said?"

"Yes." Thanks to a couple of days of ferreting out all the information I could from available sources, I'd managed to determine that the Nolan and Marie we all knew and hated had been honored by their heirs with their grandchildren's renaming. The boy and girl we'd seen in the family photo were Nolan and Marie Junior. How precious. It made me want to puke.

No doubt they were raising the brats in their own image too.

"They were in to see me over the weekend," I added, letting my tone get brisker. "It's a rather urgent matter —just got the test results back."

"I totally understand. I'll do whatever I can to help you. We do normally have that information on file—oh."

"Oh?" I asked, cocking my head and offering a wryer smile.

In spite of her earlier positive reactions to some light teasing, the secretary didn't smile back. Her brow had outright furrowed now. I could see her pulling away from me and the conversation in the tensing of her stance. "I'm afraid I won't be able to help you with this matter," she said.

Frustration prickled through my nerves. Before she could completely dismiss me, I flicked my hand across the counter and gave her a light smack to the shoulder with a quiver of supernatural energy. "Show me the computer screen without making a fuss about it."

My power didn't allow me to order her to say anything in particular, or I'd have simply commanded her to spit out what she knew. But this way worked well enough. With her mouth pressing into a strained line, she swiveled the monitor so I could see it from the other side of the counter.

The file that she'd brought up for Nolan Junior held one piece of information I'd been looking for: his enrollment date. The private school I'd determined that the Gauntt children attended started at kindergarten, but Nolan Junior, currently age ten and in fifth grade, had only started there two years ago. Which dollars to dingoes meant that he'd been adopted around that time, based on the other pieces I'd been able to assemble. There weren't many accessible facts, but those I had were starting to form a picture.

Also forming a picture, one that felt distinctly like a middle finger raised in my direction, was the window that'd popped up covering the rest of the file. *CONFIDENTIAL INFORMATION. Password required for access.*

I swatted the secretary again. "Enter the password, then."

"I can't," she said, staring at my hand as if she thought a swarm of bees might fly from my fingers next. "I don't know what it is. I've never seen this on a file before."

Fuck. It was some special security measure that the Gauntts had put in place. I gritted my teeth and gave her one last smack. "Bring up Marie Gauntt's file."

The granddaughter's profile had the same confidential message, but at least I managed to confirm that she'd also started school two years ago, one grade below her brother. The middle generation of Gauntts had adopted them both around the same time. But I didn't think they were blood siblings. They looked even less like each other than they did like their current parents.

Gritting my teeth in irritation, I dipped my head to the secretary. It wasn't her fault that the Gauntts were such pricks. And a little politeness could grease the wheels for next time... if she somehow forgot that I'd mind-controlled her into jumping to my command. "Thank you for your help."

"My pleasure," she said with a bit of a squeak, sounding surprised at her own politeness even as the words came out on autopilot.

I strode out of the building before she could decide that maybe she should call a security guard or something. For most people, the terror of something unexpected and inexplicable happening to them, something they couldn't prove or explain in any way that'd sound real to someone who hadn't experienced it, would be enough motivation to seal their lips. And if she tried to blab about a young man who'd forced her to reveal private information about students, her higher-ups would be more concerned with disciplining her than following up on her wild story.

I just wished that the effort had gotten me farther. All the time I'd spent chatting people up, conning my way into files, and making swift observations, and I knew little more than the kids' names and approximate arrival date. And none of it had led me any closer to our real goal, which was finding Lily's sister. This trumped-up daycare obviously wouldn't have been hosting brainwashed teenagers.

Thinking of Marisol, I flicked on my phone and checked the video app. New instances of the sweater challenge hashtag were starting to increase exponentially. There were less than a hundred so far, but I could tell from the momentum that it was catching on. In another couple of days, we should have thousands, and then we could hope that at least a few of them were local.

With a small sense of satisfaction, I hopped on my motorcycle and cut across town to deal with a very different sort of business. We were due for another batch of guns and ammo I'd negotiated an order for so that we could make sure our new recruits remained properly equipped. Going up against the Skeleton Corps, I didn't want us to end up with empty chambers in the middle of a shoot-out.

The black-market dealer operated out of the back

room in an Irish pub on the shady side of downtown Mayfield. The place was enough of an eyesore to make even me wince, with huge neon four-leaf clovers plastered all over the front and lime-green walls mixed with eggplant-purple tables on the inside. I'd already made a mental note never to bring Jett here or he might have a heart attack. Or a psychotic break that'd have him tearing every person in the place limb from limb.

On the other hand, I didn't always understand his artistic sensibilities. Maybe he'd have found the decor refreshingly unusual. It seemed better not to take the chance, though.

I walked straight through the bar to the back room and strode past the beaded curtain—the beads in the shape of clovers, naturally—without announcing myself. Dirk was expecting me.

Unfortunately, when he turned around from where he'd been sorting through a couple of boxes on a shelving unit behind him, I could immediately tell that he'd expected me with a whole lot of dread. His shoulders slumped, and his fingers flexed like he wished he had an AK-47 in them right now so he could blow me away and not have to deal with me at all.

That was a pretty different response from our first couple of meetings when I'd made the connection and arranged our first batch of weaponry. I hadn't known Dirk would become a dick. Something had happened.

I stepped closer so I was within punching range if need be and crossed my arms over my chest. "Have you got our loot? I have a couple of guys on the way to pick it up."

Dirk's pointed jaw twitched from side to side. "Turns out I can't do business with you lot," he said.

I arched my eyebrows. "Oh, really? And why's that? Was there some problem with the nice stack of cash I handed over last time?"

He coughed. "Your money's fine. But you don't call the shots in Mayfield. I have other... interests to consider."

He didn't have to say anything else. I could put *those* pieces together in an instant.

I had to resist the urge to clock him across the head with the gun he'd already sold me. If I needed to hit him, I could do it in a more productive way than that.

"The Skeleton Corps got to you," I said. "They told you not to sell to us anymore."

Dirk shrugged helplessly, as if he lived at the mercy of whoever jerked his chain the hardest. Which was fine. He hadn't seen how hard *we* could jerk, which was no doubt why he'd cowered at the feet of those boneheaded bozos.

"We can do this the easy way or the hard way," I told him, since it seemed only fair to give him a chance to change his mind. "Either way, you're selling us those guns. But I'd rather we did it peacefully." We had real enemies to fight. Dirk the dork wasn't one of them.

"I'm sorry," he said, splaying his hands.

I sighed. "Fine." Then I punched him in the forehead, maybe a tad harder than I totally needed to.

Supernatural energy zapped along my arm and into his brain. "Shut up and bring the boxes with the guns you were supposed to sell to us out to the car," I said. I'd learned pretty quickly that if I didn't add the first part or something similar to my commands, I had to deal with idiots yelling their heads off while they carried out my orders.

Dirk's mouth clamped shut. Wide-eyed, he turned toward the shelves and pulled down a couple of plastic crates. I grabbed one and motioned for him to take the other. We walked together to the back door, his sneakers dragging across the floor in a futile effort to keep himself from making the trek.

I'd already heard the sound of the engine in the alley out back. At least a few of the bozos on our side were punctual. When I opened the door, the new recruits were standing outside the old Bronco they drove, the doors to the cargo area popped open, bobbing on their feet like they were eager to giddy up.

"Nice!" one guy said as we carried the crates over to the back, like there was anything all that impressive about the containers themselves.

I socked Dirk in the shoulder. "Go back to your office and don't do anything else." As he trudged inside, I turned back to the other guys. "Get these back to the clubhouse immediately, and Nox'll have a bonus for you."

The other guy let out a whoop, and they both dove back into the car. As it roared off, I headed back inside.

Dirk was standing just inside the door to his office,

as commanded. I had to push him to the side so I could walk past him. Then I dug the wad of cash that was meant to be our payment out of my pocket and slapped it on the table.

"I don't have to pay you, but I am," I said, holding his frantic gaze. "I hope you'll remember that the next time you're deciding who runs things around here. You'll be able to move again in about ten minutes. Use that time to think carefully about which side you're on. I can always come back and punch you again."

A muscle in his cheek quivered. I thought his brow looked slightly damp. My instincts jangled with the sense that he knew more than what he'd admitted to already.

Thank holy hell for my observational abilities. Because of the extra sense of caution I exited the pub with, I wasn't totally surprised when three jackasses sprang at me.

The problem with trying to attack one guy when there are three of you is that you can't really all swarm him at once or you'll end up punching each other. So I simply drove my fist into the temple of the first guy who reached me and told him, "Kill the other two."

The first guy whirled around, the knife in his hand flashing, and drove it into the neck of the guy who'd been hurtling over right behind him. That guy toppled over onto the sidewalk like a beached fish, his eyes bugging out as if he couldn't believe the blood spurting out in a fountain from his carotid artery.

The third guy dodged his colleague, sputtering in

surprise. Word might have gotten around about our unusual fighting techniques, but I'd bet most of the people that word had reached had dismissed it as lies and excuses. Too bad for them—*they* weren't properly prepared.

The third guy tried to lunge at me again, but the first guy charged right at him, getting in his way. They grappled, and the knife went flying. As I pulled out my gun to solve the problem more permanently, the guy I'd instructed to murder his companions spun around and wrenched one of the metal clovers right off the window frame.

He whirled toward his former friend, slashing the clover through the air like some kind of cleaver, as if he'd become a maniacal leprechaun. I stepped back to watch the show, not seeing any reason to end it just as it was getting good.

The two men faced off with a dodge here and a feint there. The first guy raked the edge of the clover across the other guy's arm forcefully enough to cut through his shirt and draw blood. The other guy cursed at him and tried to smack the clover out of his hands like he had the knife, but his opponent wasn't falling for the same trick twice.

"Leo, you numbskull," the other guy shouted in exasperation. Leo just launched himself at him, jabbing the clover at his throat. I guessed his companion had never liked him all that much, because that was the point when the other guy took out his gun and shot Leo in the face.

Leo crumpled over, the other guy whipped toward me, and I finished off the trifecta by lodging a bullet in his skull.

The three gangsters—Skeleton Corps members, I had to assume—lay crumpled on the sidewalk. Sirens sounded in the distance thanks to some concerned citizen putting in a call after the gun shots.

It didn't matter. I'd been about to leave anyway, with as little as I had to show for my trouble. Yet again, the Corps had almost screwed us over, and we'd barely put a dent in their forces. Why couldn't I see their moves farther ahead than this?

As I shoved my pistol back into my jeans, my gaze caught on the blood still spurting from the first corpse's throat like a macabre drinking fountain. Too bad vampires weren't as real as ghosts, or one could have had a nice meal there.

The thought sunk in, and something clicked in my head. I sucked in a breath, a smile stretching across my lips. Then I raced to my bike with more speed than I usually resorted to.

The Gauntts and the Skeleton Corps had been staying ahead of us, outwitting me, far too much. But I might have just stumbled on the key that would turn the tide.

nine

Lily

When Kai brought me over to sit at the dining table with him and produced a deadly-looking paring knife, I knew I probably wasn't going to like whatever he wanted to talk to me about.

"I should have realized it sooner," he said, spinning the knife between his deft fingers like it was a baton. "You've got the power to conquer *anyone*, even the Gauntts."

"Of course she does!" Ruin said cheerfully from where he was perched on the arm of the sofa. "Next time we'll be really ready."

"That's not what I mean," Kai said with a mildly irritated tone.

Nox spun one of the other dining chairs around and sat on it with his arms folded over the top. "Well, why don't you get on with telling us about your new genius idea, then?"

As Jett drifted over from the kitchen and leaned against the wall to watch, Kai rolled up his sleeves to his elbows. The light brown skin beneath was smooth with a dusting of fine hairs.

"I was thinking," he said, looking up at me, "about your trick with the coffee. And your beer attack in the fight the other day. And it occurred to me, way later than it should have, that blood is something like ninety percent water."

A tendril of nausea unfurled in my gut as I caught on to the implications. No, I definitely didn't like the direction this conversation was going in.

"Kai," I started, my instinctive revulsion tickling up through my chest.

"Listen," he insisted. "This could be the answer to everything. Taking on the Gauntts and the Skeleton Corps too if you want to lend us a hand there. Even finding your sister. You and she share the same bloodline, after all. If you can control blood, then you control *life*. But first we need to test my theory out and make sure I'm not blowing hot air."

"Any more than usual," Jett muttered, but he was eyeing us with open curiosity now.

"Fuck," Nox said. "*I* should have thought of that."

Ruin clapped his hands together, his eyes gleaming. "Lily's going to sock it to those rich pricks with their own blood!"

"We don't even know if I can," I protested. "And how can we experiment that won't—"

Kai didn't bother answering with words. He just brought the knife to his arm and cut a shallow line through his skin, about an inch long.

My stomach lurched again. Tiny beads of blood seeped out along the thin cut. He hadn't even winced, so I guessed it hadn't hurt that much. But still. He was carving himself open so I could conduct this experiment. Even if he wanted to see the results as much as anyone, that didn't seem right.

And what if I screwed this up somehow? It wasn't as if I had perfect control even over water. At least if I created an accidental tidal wave, all that would happen was some people getting wet. Blood... Blood was something else entirely.

Like Kai had said, it was life. And now it was his life I'd be playing with.

I swallowed thickly. Kai met my eyes again, his expression showing nothing but confident anticipation. "Give it a shot, Lily. Be the barracuda you know you can be. Make a little art."

The eagerness in his tone and the way he phrased it dampened my disgust just a little. I eyed the droplets of blood that had formed along the cut and dragged in a breath.

Move them around a little. Find out whether I *could*

direct them to my will. There wasn't anything so horrible about just testing out that possibility, was there? It wasn't as if I were going to reach out to the rest of the blood inside him. The loss of a few specks obviously hadn't killed him.

Hell, even taking a bullet to his brain hadn't *totally* killed him twenty-one years ago.

My churning emotions had stirred the hum in my chest. I didn't want to rile it up as much as I had in the past. I didn't need to mess around with the blood a *lot* to be sure I could actually affect it. Baby steps seemed like the safest approach.

I set my hand on the tabletop and drummed a soft rhythm with my fingertips, letting that beat and the thump of my heart steady me. Then I focused on the beads of blood and threw a little of that supernatural energy at them, willing them to move toward me.

The second my power touched the ruddy liquid, I felt it resonate with the hum inside me. The drops streaked a couple of inches across Kai's arm toward me, leaving a thin red train in their wake.

A grin split Kai's face. "I was right. You're going to rule them all. You'll be fucking unstoppable."

I let my hand go still, the hum dwindling inside me. My revulsion had faded, but trepidation had taken up residence in my gut in its place. "How? You want me to go around calling people's blood right out of their bodies or something?"

I'd watched the guys commit more than one murder in self-defense… I'd helped them in small ways from the sidelines. But I'd never taken a life myself. The thought of doing it, especially in a way I had to think would be horribly painful—getting the blood wrung out of you while you were alive to feel it?—left me chilled.

"If they deserve it, why the fuck not?" Nox said with a smirk.

Kai shot him a baleful look. "I was thinking of something a little more elegant. No need for you to make a mess if you don't want to. I'd imagine with a little practice you could get to the point where you could send all the blood in a person's body toward their heart and burst it right inside their chest. Neat and contained but gets the job done just fine."

I still felt shivery at the thought, but at the same time, picturing Nolan Gauntt's coolly patronizing face, imagining how his expression would clench with fear as I pummeled his heart with his own blood, gave me a dark sort of thrill.

Could I really do that? And if I could... he really wouldn't be able to stop me, would he?

No matter what powers he had, no one could survive without their heart.

"Give it another try," Kai said, bringing his gaze back to me. His eyes gleamed behind the panes of his glasses. "Draw a little out. I've got plenty to spare. I want to see how much you can do."

I stared at his arm, caught in a weird mix of uneasiness and excitement. The other three guys leaned a little closer in anticipation. I thought of Nolan Gauntt again, of how he'd wrenched my sister away from me just when I'd gotten her out from under Mom's and Wade's thumbs, and the hum reverberated through my chest at a higher pitch.

Wetting my lips, I let my fingers fall back into their steady rhythm against the tabletop. Just a little. Just a little of the blood pulsing through Kai's veins, called out to trickle across his skin. I could do that, couldn't I? I had so much more control over my powers already than I'd had just a few weeks ago.

I tugged at the liquid coursing through his arm with my mind and a quiver of supernatural energy. A speckling of more blood bubbled along the little cut. It formed into a narrow ribbon that dribbled over the curve of his forearm. A metallic taste formed in the back of my mouth, and a heady sense of power rushed through me.

Unfortunately, that rush sent me off balance. As the thrill expanded inside me, I yanked harder than I'd meant to, and a whole spurt of scarlet liquid gushed from the cut to splatter on the dining table.

I yelped, my connection to Kai's pulse shattering. There was a stack of paper napkins left on the table after our last takeout meal. I snatched a handful and pressed them to Kai's arm, even though as far as I could tell the stream of blood had tapered off as soon as I'd withdrawn my control.

Kai curled his fingers around my own arm and gave me a comforting squeeze. No sign of pain showed on his face. "It's okay. It was only a little jolt. I'm perfectly fine."

How could he be so calm?

I grimaced at him. "I don't want to hurt you."

Kai let out a low chuckle that sent a different type of electricity tingling low in my belly. He slid forward on his chair and reached for my other hand. "You don't have to worry about that. Watching you work is having the opposite effect."

I didn't know what he meant until he brought my hand to his groin. My palm came to rest on the unmistakable bulge of an erection. Kai's eyelids dipped, heavy with lust, and all of me flushed, from my cheeks down to my core.

"I'm pretty sure I didn't send any blood flowing *there*," I couldn't help saying. It was impossible not to rub my hand up and down the length of him through his jeans, even more heat racing through me at the concrete evidence of his lustful appreciation.

Kai let out a softly urgent noise and pulled me right onto his lap. He ran his hands up into my hair. "You sent it there just by being your incredible self. You can pull the life right out of me as easily as fucking *breathing*. Do you have any idea what a turn-on that is?"

I wouldn't have thought of it as one, but I couldn't really argue with the bulge of his cock now pressing between my legs or his fingers tracing scorching lines over my scalp—or the kiss he pulled me into.

His lips seared against mine, devouring me. His fingers tangled in my hair and tugged hard enough to bring out pinpricks of pain that sparked pleasure at the same time.

EVA CHASE

I whimpered, and he smiled against my mouth. Then his tongue swept in to tease over mine, his hands trailing down the sides of my body alongside the kiss. He paused to sweep his fingers over my breasts and then drew them lower to squeeze my ass, pulling me even tighter against him. The feel of him rigidly hard against my sex had me grinding against him, desperate for more.

Kai tipped his head back just far enough to whip off his glasses and toss them onto the table with a clatter, and I became abruptly aware of our audience. The other three Skullbreakers were still in the room, of course.

Nox had gotten up from his chair. His gaze branded my skin, smoldering with an intoxicating combination of hunger and possessiveness. Ruin had sucked his lower lip under his teeth in a way that made me want to go over and kiss him. His eyes sparkled with nothing but enthusiastic desire. And Jett…

Jett remained in his pose leaning against the wall, his shoulders tensed and his expression rigid. But he hadn't torn his attention away from me.

Kai flicked a glance around at the others. "There's plenty of Lily to go around," he said casually. "No need to just stand there." Then he yanked my mouth back to his.

As we kissed, he squeezed my ass again and then dipped one hand between us to stroke my clit through my pants. Bliss shot through me in a crackling bolt, and I outright moaned. Whatever new dimensions to my powers we'd uncovered, they couldn't be all that bad if they made Kai want to do this to me, could they?

And not just him. Nox's massive presence loomed beside me, his mouth seeking out the side of my neck. As his lips marked a blazing trail down the side to the crook of my shoulder, he reached around to cup both my breasts at the same time. I rocked into Kai's hand and arched my back to meet Nox's caresses, delight washing through me in a torrent.

When Kai drew back, his breath was coming rough. "Take her shirt off," he told Nox. I'd noticed he got bossy when he was in makeout mode. But I wasn't complaining.

Neither was Nox. He chuckled and peeled my sweater right off me. Then he unclasped my bra for good measure. As he slid his hands over my breasts skin to skin, tweaking my nipples so I gasped, Ruin stepped up at my other side.

"Our gorgeous, mighty Waterlily," he murmured, and captured my mouth next.

Even being with two guys before had been a novel experience. Three had my thoughts completely spiraling in a whirlwind of shared desire. I ran my hands down Kai's chest and yanked his own shirt up, figuring the nakedness shouldn't go just one way.

As Ruin shifted his kisses to my jaw and then my earlobe with a light nibble, Nox hummed approvingly. "Going to be a good girl for Kai too, aren't you?" he murmured in that voice that instantly turned me to putty.

I circled my hands over Kai's taut nipples and smiled at the genius. "I think Kai likes me better naughty."

Kai let out a heated laugh at the callback to our first hookup and dipped his hand right inside my pants to stroke me more effectively. "Hell yes, I do."

"You can be good at being naughty then," Nox insisted, and lowered his head to claim the other side of my neck while he kept working over my breasts.

I palmed Kai's erection again, and a new hunger spread through my chest, making my mouth water. I knew just how I could be *very* good at naughtiness.

I pushed myself back off his lap and eased to the floor between his splaying knees. As I reached for the button of his fly, Jett let out a curt sound. He shoved off the wall and stalked across the room to the front door, which shut with a thump in his wake.

I hesitated, my stomach twisting, my gaze glued to the door. Nox guided my attention back to the three of them with two fingers under my chin.

"Don't worry about our tortured artist," he said. "He'll sort himself out eventually. What did you have in mind for the rest of us, Siren?"

I glanced up at Kai. A flush had crept up his neck, and he licked his lips. Without prompting, he flicked open the fly of his jeans.

I wanted him. I wanted all of them. That had nothing to do with Jett and whatever the hell *he* wanted. He wasn't into watching or joining in? That was fine. It shouldn't stop me from enjoying myself with the men who were sure of their desires.

I tugged Kai's jeans down his hips and freed his rigid cock from his boxers. Just the pump of my fingers had him groaning.

"Fuck, Lily," he said, his head tipping back in the chair. "Go ahead and eat me alive." He narrowed his eyes at Nox and Ruin. "Make sure she gets off plenty too."

Nox snorted. "Like we'd somehow forget the best part."

As I leaned forward to wrap my lips around the heat of Kai's shaft, Nox took over where his friend had been teasing my clit before. Not content to work around my clothes, he tugged my pants and panties down to my knees. Then he stroked his fingers between my legs with a growl as he felt how wet I was.

I sucked Kai's cock deeper into my mouth, loving the way it twitched at the swirl of my tongue and how his breath hitched at the same time. He was so rarely anything but self-controlled, it felt like some kind of magic to unravel him like this.

As Kai massaged my scalp with encouraging fingers, Ruin slipped beneath me and closed his lips around one of my nipples. He suckled me alongside the pulsing of Nox's hand against my sex until I was moaning my pleasure over Kai.

"I think you're ready for more," Nox said, slipping a finger and then two right inside me. "You can take all of us so good, can't you? Someday we'll fill you to the brim. For now…"

There was a crinkle of foil, and then his cock pressed against my slit. As he pushed into me, filling me with an ecstatic burn, I closed my mouth around Kai's shaft so tightly my teeth grazed the silky skin. Kai's hips jerked up, a curse tumbling from his lips that was all lustful abandon.

Ruin dipped his head lower, nibbling across my belly until he reached the mound of my sex. Without any apparent concern about Nox's cock thrusting in and out of me just a fraction of an inch away, he lapped his tongue across my clit.

A cry I couldn't contain burst out of me. I clamped my mouth around Kai again, but I was lost, swept away on the flood of pleasure coursing through me.

Nox filled me again and again with a slight swivel of his hips that sent me even higher, and Ruin sucked on my clit, and Kai nicked my scalp with his fingernails— and I was coming, breaking apart and melding together and then melting all over again with the heat surging through my nerves.

I sucked hard on Kai's cock, and he erupted into my mouth with a salty gush I didn't mind at all. I swallowed it down through my gasps.

"You milk both of us so sweet," Nox muttered, and then his hips jerked as he groaned. My sex clenched around his final thrusts, which sent me soaring all over again.

Limp with satisfaction, I sagged against the front of

Kai's chair, looping one hand around his leg. Ruin nuzzled my temple with a pleased murmur that showed he didn't mind at all that he hadn't gotten any release from this encounter. Nox hunkered down next to me and tucked me onto his lap, letting me keep my hand on Kai's leg.

"Our woman," he said proudly. "No one's but ours. The rest of the world better watch the fuck out."

ten

Lily

A cool fall breeze teased through my hair as I peered at the tall brick apartment buildings around us. "Why are we starting here?"

When Kai had come hustling out of the bedroom this morning with his latest brilliant brainstorm on his lips, suggesting that maybe I could use my new blood magic to track down Marisol as well, I hadn't wanted to waste any time. Which meant he hadn't had much chance to explain all the particulars before he'd headed off to work. He'd called Nox a couple of times as he'd thought the idea through, and we'd set off shortly afterward.

Now, Nox chuckled. "Mr. Know-It-All had some complex explanation for why he thought this was the best spot. Something about it being halfway between the Thrivewell building and your apartment where your sister went running from, and typical kidnapping patterns and a bunch of other stuff. I bet if you text him, he'll lay it out in full detail."

Jett let out a disgruntled groan from where he was sitting astride his motorcycle. "Can we skip that part?"

When I glanced over at the artist, a wobbly twinge ran through my gut. He looked like his usual gruffly taciturn self, but I couldn't tell whether he was just a normal level of grouchy or "I'm peeved because I saw you making out with my buddies last night" grouchy. And if it was the latter, I wasn't sure what I could do to make it better.

"I think we'd better skip it," I said quickly. "Kai's at work; I don't want to distract him."

At least while he was at the Thrivewell building, he'd been able to confirm that the Gauntts had arrived on schedule and therefore were nowhere near my sister. Unless they had her stashed away in one of their offices, which seemed unlikely.

Ruin bobbed eagerly on his feet. "It doesn't matter where we start. Now your blood can lead us right to her! And then we'll show those assholes what's what."

I looked down at my arms, picturing the blood pulsing through my arteries and veins. "We don't know for sure that it'll work yet. It was just a theory."

"When Kai comes up with a theory, it's practically fact," Nox said. "Come on, let's give it a shot. You've got your inspiration?"

"Yeah." I pulled a T-shirt I'd taken from Marisol's suitcase out of my purse. When I held it to my face, a faint whiff of the sugary perfume she'd started wearing sometime in her teens filled my nose.

I closed my eyes and pictured her the last time I'd hugged her. The feel of her fragile body in my embrace. The joy that had shone in her face when I'd escorted her into the apartment. The awe that'd threaded through her voice when she'd taken in her room, visions of how she'd decorate it sparking in her eyes.

I thought of other things too: the farting unicorns and ditzy dragons she'd used to draw, the goofy games we used to play down by the marsh, picking bits of grass and reeds out of her hair afterward. And the last time I'd seen her, happily chowing down on pancakes and then hurling accusations at me.

All of those pieces formed my experience of my sister. I had to soak myself in the impressions of her like they were a salt bath, until all the essence of her I could collect had permeated my pores. Maybe it'd do my complexion some good too.

With each image, the hum of power inside me rose, wrapping around a pang of loss and worry. What had happened to her after she'd run from the apartment? How was she now? Had the Gauntts hurt her—more than they already had when she was younger? Was she even still alive?

That last question heightened the hum into an outright roar. I focused on the energy resonating through my body and my sense of my little sister flowing alongside it, all tangled together by the pounding of my pulse.

Find her, I thought, not totally sure who I was aiming the command at. *Find the girl whose blood matches mine better than anyone else in the world. Feel all the little pieces of DNA that fit with hers racing through my veins and reach out until you touch their echo.*

It might have been a good theory, but Kai hadn't been totally sure how it would work in a concrete sense. He'd told me to try whatever occurred to me to get in touch with my awareness of my sister, to stir up the commonalities in my blood that I might be able to sense in hers as well using my weird watery powers. I'd never tried to find anyone or anything with my magic before. It wasn't like we needed a search party to locate the lake.

"Is it working?" Ruin asked in a hopeful hush.

I didn't open my eyes, but I could tell from the soft smack of sound that Nox had swatted him. "Let her concentrate."

I didn't have any sense of direction yet. I shifted my weight on my feet, groping for other ways I could shape the power inside me to my intention. I had to hone it to the qualities I shared with Marisol, the common elements that filled our blood... How the hell did I do that? I was a mailroom clerk, not a geneticist.

On an impulse, I started to move, my sneakers rasping against the sidewalk. I kept my eyes shut, but I trusted that the guys wouldn't let me walk into traffic. I swayed and spun and swept my arms through the air,

105

mimicking the wild dances we'd played out as kids as I pictured them behind my eyelids.

I probably looked like some kind of manic mime to anyone passing by, but they could shove their judgments where the sun didn't shine. I just wanted to find my sister.

The rhythm of my strange dance brought the other melodies flowing through me into tight focus. The rumble of passing cars and the hiss of the breeze over a nearby awning blended into it. A tingle filled my throat with the urge to put words to it, but an ache closed around the sensation an instant later.

No singing. Not while she was gone. I couldn't bring myself to do it.

I threw myself faster into the dance instead. The wind whirled around me. A quiver ran through the hum inside me—and latched on to my heart with a hint of a tug.

"That way," I murmured. With a leap of my pulse, I swiveled in the direction the tug seemed to be drawing me and pointed.

Nox didn't wait for further instructions. He plucked me off the ground and plopped me on the back of his motorcycle, hopping on in front of me. As he started the engine, I wrapped one hand around his chest and kept the other tracing memories in the air. With the thrum of the motor vibrating through the bike's frame, the tug inside me pulled harder.

Nox took off, not too fast, following my gesture. I kept my eyes closed, but I heard the other two guys set off alongside us. Marisol danced on inside my mind, and I set her movements to the tempo of my heartbeat.

So much of the same blood coursed through her body as it did mine. I needed to reach out to it. Needed to let it draw me to her. Please.

The tug yanked at me again. "There!" I said, jabbing my finger into the air again. I didn't dare look to see where we were going for fear I'd break the spell I'd conjured inside me.

Nox veered left, and my body swayed with his. The other bikes careened after us. The wind whipped over me, nipping at my clothes, but I didn't care. Joy was expanding inside me.

I was doing it. I was following the familial thread between me and my sister like it was a fishing line and I was reeling myself in to her.

The tug shifted. I switched arms, trailing the other through the air. Someone must have made a rude gesture in response, because Nox shouted out, "I bet your mom likes that!" My lips twitched with an unbidden smile.

The pull inside me was getting stronger, my pulse seeming to thump louder through my chest and skull with every passing second. We had to be getting closer. Where had the Gauntts hidden her away? What had they told her?

It didn't matter. I had to get her away from them, and then we could sort out the rest. As long as she was in their clutches, nothing else mattered.

A faint whine formed inside my ears, like the drone

of a mosquito. I restrained myself from swatting at the non-existent insect and focused as well as I could on the image of my sister in my head. I poked my finger one way and another, tipping here and there with the swerve of the bike.

And then the tug started to fade. It dwindled in my grasp as if it were a candle on the verge of guttering. I clutched at it as well as I could with my mental faculties, but it kept waning, slipping through my fingers.

"Faster!" I called to Nox over the warble of the wind. "I think they're moving her. Maybe they noticed that we're getting close."

"Which way?" he shouted back to me, gunning the engine.

I felt for that place inside me that'd steered me right before, but I'd lost my sense of direction. The tug was so faint now it was only the vague impression that she was somewhere in the vicinity, not too close.

Alive. She was definitely alive. For a few minutes there, I'd almost tasted the rhythm of her own pulse thumping alongside mine.

"I don't know," I had to admit. "She's moving away too quickly."

Nox tore through the streets, chasing what amounted to a phantom. Although I guessed that was appropriate for a guy who'd been a ghost until about a month ago. My pulse raced on, and Marisol bobbed and dipped in her childhood prancing in my mind's eye, but I got nothing more than a chalky flavor seeping through my mouth.

Finally I shook my head against Nox's back. He eased the bike to a halt. I opened my eyes and found myself staring up at the garish window display for Kids Paradise Toy Superstore. The bug-eyed dolls and neon plushies staring out at us felt like an insult to our quest. What kind of kid actually wanted those nightmares in their house?

Better those than one of the Gauntts, I had to admit.

"What happened?" Ruin asked, hurrying over from his own bike.

I let him help me off of Nox's motorcycle and rubbed my forehead. The beat of my pulse had sharpened into a headache.

"I'm not sure," I said. "I thought I felt her—I thought we were going toward her. But then it all kind of washed away, like she was getting so far I couldn't reach her anymore. But maybe I imagined all of it. Stranger things have happened." The three guys standing around me were ample proof of that fact.

"The Gauntts could have eyes all over the city," Jett pointed out. "They don't want you finding her."

"They don't know about her secret powers yet," Ruin said.

"They don't," I agreed. "But they'd still be able to see if we're closing in on them one way or another." I leaned into him, exhaustion rolling over me that was even more difficult to fight off than the throbbing behind my temples.

Ruin pressed a gentle kiss to the back of my head. "Then we try again when they *can't* see us," he said.

Jett snorted at the simplistic-sounding suggestion, but as it sank into my weary brain, I had to say it made a certain kind of sense. If we went about our search in a stealthier way instead of charging around the city in broad daylight, we'd have a better chance of getting close enough to get to Marisol before the Gauntts' minions caught on.

I wrapped one hand around Ruin's arm and the other around Nox's. "Okay. Next time we'll try at night. And if any of the Gauntts are with her then… I have plenty of ways of dealing with them."

Nox smirked. "Now that's what I like to hear, Minnow. We're coming up behind them, and soon they'll have no idea what hit them."

eleven

Jett

I scratched the pencil across the sketch pad propped on my lap, wincing at the hissing sound the tip made on the paper and the spidery lines left in its wake. I vastly preferred working my medium into my canvas directly with my fingers, but of course that didn't allow for the finer details I sometimes felt the need to accentuate.

I glanced up from the armchair toward the sofa, where Lily had curled up with a book, her legs tucked next to her on the cushions. Theoretically, she was unwinding from the stresses of the day by doing some reading. But while I wasn't as observant as our know-it-all Kai, even I couldn't help noticing she was only turning a page about once every five minutes. A couple of times she'd actually flipped backward, like she was reading in reverse.

I wasn't much of a book fanatic either, but that didn't seem to bode well.

She'd wanted to go out looking for her sister again tonight, but her earlier attempt at wrangling her blood had left her too wiped out. We'd gone outside, deciding to start from the apartment where she'd last seen her sister this time, but she hadn't been able to summon any of the connection she'd felt before. After a few tries, whirling and swaying on the sidewalk in increasingly frantic imitations of what she'd said were the childhood dances they played in, she'd crumpled like a marionette with its strings cut.

Thankfully, Nox had caught her before she'd smacked into anything. Then he'd ordered her to rest until tomorrow and carried her upstairs to the apartment before she could get out more than a few words in argument.

I didn't let myself look closely at the twinge that came into my chest at remembering her nestled in his arms. I had a whole lot of other twinges running through me every time I looked at her anyway. Some of them were acceptable.

We'd found new ways she could use her powers, new strategies for sticking it to the Gauntts, but how much more was this fight going to take out of her before we reached the end?

Were we even going to reach the end, or were we going to drag her down in our own war instead of raising her up the way we'd intended when we first barged back into town?

I didn't have the answers to either of those questions, so I drained the last of my cola, letting the sugar rush wash a little of my apprehension away, and added a few more lines to the page. When I'd captured the curve of her chin and the bend of her knee, I set the pencil aside and reached for my ink pad. It offered up enough colors to satisfy me without much mess, so it worked best for smaller portraits like this.

I could have used my supernatural powers on the paper and brought out colors that way, but somehow that seemed like cheating. Anyway, I shouldn't exhaust my own voodoo energies on something I could do just as well, if not better, through my regular methods.

As I finished adding the smudge of blue to her hair and started filling out her shirt, Lily shifted on the couch and lifted her arms over her head in a stretch. My gaze immediately shot to her, taking in the way her body filled out her shirt with its soft curves. Soft curves I could still remember pressing up against my chest.

Heat flooded me, condensing in my groin. In an instant, I was half-mast. My jaw clenched against the sensation, but my dick didn't really care how annoyed I was with it.

Drawing her had been a bad idea. At least right now when my control was still so frayed from that early-morning interlude. I *had* to be able to work with her image again sometime. What was the point in having a muse if I couldn't commit her own form to canvas?

Standing up abruptly, I closed the sketchpad and dropped it next to the inks on the side table I'd claimed as mine. Then I stalked into the bedroom that technically belonged to all four of us Skullbreakers.

Going in there might have been a bad idea. The Murphy bed where I'd lain next to Lily last week was raised, and we'd brought in a dresser and a chair and a stack of motorcycle parts Nox planned on beefing up his ride with, so it didn't look much like the room had that night. But the hazy glow of streetlamp light filtering past the window, which we still didn't have a curtain for, brought back the memories twice as clearly.

I turned away from the window and focused on the mural I'd been creating on the far wall—the only wall that didn't have any furniture against it at the moment. It contained the door to the closet, but I'd been incorporating that into my vague sense of the design. The paints I'd been using swerved and flowed across the surface in something that might have been a flash flood or a hurricane, blues and purples and oranges twining and colliding. But here and there, little pockets of calm had emerged. I was still figuring out what each would contain.

As I took the image in, a tingle of inspiration gripped me. I grabbed one of the little cans of paint off the top of the dresser, popped the lid, and dipped two fingers in.

With the stroke of my hand, the red flared like a beam of ruddy light out of the whorl I'd focused on. It was brighter than the reds I usually preferred, but that seemed to fit here. Maybe I'd add a little of my blood to the mix to shade it, if that felt right once I'd captured the shape tugging at my mind completely.

I'd finished streaking tendrils and dappling some of the surrounding area with faint dabs of the same red and was just wiping my fingers off on a rag when Lily slipped into the room.

She paused just inside the doorway when she saw me, a smile lighting her face as she took in my work. Suddenly, I couldn't smell the tang of the paint anymore, only her sweetly aquatic scent. Every inch of my skin thrummed with awareness of how close she was standing, just a couple of feet away—and how much certain parts of me wanted to close that distance.

The other guys went to her so easily. But that was exactly why I shouldn't. I wasn't just one more jerk in the crowd.

And if I let myself get lost in Lily that way, I wasn't sure how much else I'd let slip from my grasp. What mistakes I might make. Being *that* close to her, absorbing her with my hands and mouth as well as my eyes, had brought out emotions far too close to the ones that'd overwhelmed me at the worst possible time before, only even more intense.

The draw I felt toward her was dangerous—for everyone around me more than for myself. I wasn't going to be selfish this time.

So I unfocused my eyes slightly, doing my best to transform the woman before me into a more abstract smattering of shapes like I viewed everyone outside my inner circle. I couldn't quite reduce her to mere blobs of color, but I let my vision of her melt and slide until I pictured her more like a Dali, warped features running amuck. There was nothing particularly appealing about that.

If my dick still twitched a little, I was just going to pretend it hadn't.

"Hey," Lily said, biting her lip, which I was currently imagining about half a foot to the right of her nose. "This is looking really amazing."

I jerked my gaze back to the mural. Next to her, even with the Dali treatment I'd given her, the sprawling landscape of paint looked flat and lifeless. But she saw something in it. I could tell from her tone that she wasn't just bullshitting the way most people did when they talked about art, complimenting the things they thought they should like and making awkward commentary on the rest.

"It isn't done," I felt the need to say. I wasn't sure how long it would take before I felt it'd gotten there. Maybe it never would. There were few pieces I'd actually felt fully satisfied with in my life... Possibly not any since I'd met Lily.

Not because she dragged me down. Oh, no, not at all. She'd given me a higher standard to aspire to, and every part of me ached with the desire to meet it. That was what a good muse brought you—ambition and vision.

I just had to prove myself worthy of those gifts.

"Well, hopefully we'll be here long enough for you

to get it to a place where you're happy with it." Lily tilted her head to the side as her gaze traveled across the expanse of color. "I think it's spectacular already, so it's going to be absolutely breathtaking when you're finished with it."

"I'm glad you think so," I said gruffly, not having any words more adequate than those to express my appreciation.

Lily hesitated, ducking her head briefly. Then she said, "Can I talk to you a little? There's something I figure you'll understand better than the other guys, but if I'm interrupting you…"

Her uncertainty wrenched at me. That she thought she had to ask permission just to have a conversation with me—like I might shove her aside for daring to do more than praise my artwork—

But then, I *had* shoved her aside already. Well, really, I'd been shoving myself away from her, but it'd have amounted to the same thing from her perspective, wouldn't it?

"Of course," I said quickly, forcing myself to turn toward her and hold her gaze again, even though that was more difficult when I was imagining one of her eyes sliding down her cheek and the other up into her forehead. "What's up?"

"I just…" She leaned back against the side of the dresser, her lips twisting into a frown. "I don't know how you feel about your art, but I'm guessing it's at least kind of similar to how I feel about singing. Like there's something inside you that's just there, wanting to get out. Like you have things to say that just talking couldn't manage. If that makes any sense."

I couldn't stop warmth from blooming in my chest at how well she'd described the impulses that'd guided me since I was a kid. "It makes total sense. That's exactly what it's like."

"Okay. Then I don't sound crazy. At least in that one specific way." She let out a rough giggle and combed one hand through her hair, making the blue-dyed streaks tumble against her shoulder like a trickling tropical waterfall. Suddenly I was picturing pushing up against her under a waterfall like that, pinning her to a slick rock and kissing her with salt lacing our lips—

My dick started to rise again, and I jerked my mind back to the present. Giving myself a mental smack, I amped the Dali-ness up to 100. Now one of her eyes was stacked on top of the other, and her chin was halfway across the room.

She was still fucking gorgeous, damn it.

"I still have that feeling inside me," she was saying. "And I hear rhythms and melodies around me that I want to add a song to. But if I try to, the words just catch in my throat. I couldn't sing for ages after I got shipped off to the psych hospital, but it started to come back after you guys found me... Then I lost Marisol again, and it's like it's all locked up inside me. I can't find a way to let it out. I'm not sure... I'm not sure I even deserve to."

Her voice dropped to a whisper with those last words. My throat constricted. In spite of my intentions,

I stepped toward her, letting myself touch her shoulder with a squeeze that was as gentle and reassuring as I could manage. "You deserve everything," I told her.

Lily gave me a smile I could tell was sad even though I'd distorted her face into a jumble in my head. "But if it's something I'm really meant to do, if singing *is* art for me and not just a silly thing I do, shouldn't it always come? You've never stopped making art. You were *dead* for two decades, and you started up as soon as you got back." She rubbed her temple. "That's not the point, though. Obviously you can't tell me what I'm meant to be doing. Mostly I'm just babbling. I thought you might have some idea how maybe I could let it out again, or you'd say I shouldn't even try, or—I don't know."

I was sharply aware of the heat of her body seeping into my palm through her shirt, but I didn't move my hand. I couldn't, not when she was making this appeal to me. To *me*, not Nox the boss or Ruin the comforter or Kai the genius.

And it could be that she'd been right to. There were things I could tell her, even if I wasn't sure how much they'd help.

I opened my mouth, and the words stuck in my own throat. I didn't talk about this stuff. Some of it I didn't even like admitting to myself. But if Lily was my muse, I should be open with her. I should be able to tell her anything, at least when it came to that side of myself.

"I'm always making art," I said, "but that doesn't

mean it always feels like I'm really getting what's inside me out onto the canvas—or wall or whatever. What you're talking about, I kind of feel that way all the time, no matter how much I smear paint around on paper."

Lily's brow knit. "What do you mean? You make fantastic stuff." She motioned to the wall.

"But it's not quite—" I paused, sorting through my thoughts to find the best way of explaining it.

"My parents were shit," I started again. "Like, I'm not even shocked by the crap we're finding out about the Gauntts and the kids they messed with, because as far as I'm concerned that's just what people are like. There wasn't a day when they didn't hurl insults at me and find some excuse to slap me across the head or kick the legs out from under me. That was life in our house. You never knew when the next blow would come. It didn't even need to have a reason."

I looked down at my other hand and curled my fingers into a fist. When I was big enough, I'd started giving them the same treatment in return. And not just them. There was a lot more in me than just art that sometimes screamed to be let out.

Lily reached up to set her hand over mine on her shoulder. "I'm so sorry, Jett."

I shrugged. "It's over now. I hadn't seen them in years even before I died. It's part of who I am. But that part…" I swallowed and met her eyes again. "I can let the art out, yeah. But it hardly ever feels totally right. Sometimes I think I'm just too messed up, too many broken pieces in there, for it to ever come together the way it should. I know where I want to get to, but I can't quite reach it, and maybe that's how it'll always be."

Unfairly, I expected her to murmur soothing words that I wouldn't believe about how that couldn't possibly be true. Instead, she pulled me into an unexpected hug. Suddenly her body was pressed against mine, her arms wrapped around me, and I could barely think at all.

"If there are parts of you that are messed up, then that's who you are too," she said. "And that's fine. Art can be messed up, right? It's not supposed to be neat and tidy. And whatever you make, it's still *yours*. Even if it isn't exactly perfect, I think that's still way better than someone who makes some painting that's practically a photocopy and gets every detail right, but their soul isn't in it at all."

I let my arms ease around her, my eyes sliding shut just for a moment. I didn't know if what she was saying was right, but I could tell her this much. "Maybe. But my point is that you don't think I'm not an artist just because I know I'm not doing everything I'd want to. So having trouble singing the way *you* want to doesn't mean you aren't one either. If there's something in you that's broken, we'll fix it as well as we can. We'll get your sister back. And if you need more than that, we'll figure it out too."

I heard the bob of her throat, drank in her scent, and then she was easing back from me—carefully, respectfully, like she didn't want to cross my boundaries. She had no idea that right now my body was clamoring to do nothing less than toss her up on top of that dresser and bury my face between her thighs until she was moaning my name.

"Thank you," she said. "I don't know how that's all going to work… but everything is definitely easier now that I'm not alone. We just need to make sure that Marisol isn't alone either."

"We'll find her," I said firmly. And if we couldn't, if the Gauntts had somehow torn her too far away from Lily for us to ever recover her, then those pricks would find themselves shredded like fucking coleslaw.

Lily gave me one last smile, a little brighter than before, and I couldn't look away as she drifted back out into the living room. Not until I noticed Nox standing by the windows, watching us.

His gaze caught mine, and his mouth curved into one of its knowing smirks, like he knew exactly what I'd been imagining. Like it mattered.

I scowled at him and shut the door.

twelve

Lily

It looked like the guys had put enough of the fear of God—or at least the fear of the Skullbreakers—into the first Skeleton Corps group they'd tackled, because none of them had tattled on us. The man we were expecting showed up behind the convenience store promptly on schedule.

Too bad for him, the squad he was supposed to give orders to wasn't waiting for him, and the Skullbreakers were.

"Who the hell—" he snapped out as the four guys burst from the shadows, and that was all he managed to say before Kai had clocked him across the head with an order to "Shut up and stay where you are."

The man went rigid as a telephone pole. He

appeared to be a bit older than the bunch we'd tackled before, no gray in his hair or anything like that, but his features were hardened beyond any hint of boyishness. I figured he was around thirty. That seemed to bode well for him having a little more authority than the others.

"What now?" Jett asked, stalking around the guy. "I'm guessing he's not going to cough up who *he* works under just like that."

The Corps guy just glared at him, looking like he was trying to spew all the threats he'd have liked to be making out of his eyes instead of his mouth.

Nox glanced the guy up and down and said with typical confidence, "I don't think beating him into submission will work any better than it did on the others. Ruin, how about an attitude adjustment?"

Ruin grinned and stepped forward with his fists raised. He paused for a moment as if deciding exactly what kind of attitude he'd like to convey and then pummeled our captive in the shoulder.

Apparently one burst of supernatural energy overrode the previous. The man stumbled to the side and moved to catch his balance, the motionless spell Kai had put him under broken. Then his eyes flashed. Before I could worry that Ruin had miscalculated and made the guy even more pissed off at us, he spun and started barreling out of the alley.

Nox charged after him. "Where the fuck are you going?"

"To teach those pricks who've been bossing me around a lesson," the guy snapped, and I understood.

Ruin had made him furious—with his own colleagues. Furious enough to want to go confront them right now. And unlike the last guys, he seemed to know where they were.

Nox waved for us to follow, and we all hustled over to the motorcycles they'd parked nearby. The guy dove into his car like he was rushing off to carry out life-saving surgery instead of to yell at his fellow gangsters.

He zoomed off down the street, and we took off after him, following close behind. There was no need to keep a low profile when he didn't care about anything at the moment other than letting loose a few rants.

The guy didn't drive far, only to a pawn shop with a closed sign on the door. Driven by Ruin's inflicted fury, he ignored the sign, yanking at the knob so hard he managed to bust the lock.

"What the hell, man?" a voice hollered from inside.

The man burst into the shop. In the few seconds it took us to hurry in after him, he managed to shatter an entire tea set by hurling it at the guy who'd been cashing out behind the counter, slamming the pot into his head just as we got inside. It didn't look like the set had been anything all that nice anyway, so maybe that was the most appropriate use for it.

The guy he was attacking had cringed backward with his hands raised. "What the fuck's gotten into you, you lunatic?" he demanded.

"We have," Nox announced, and gestured to his men. Kai punched the first guy with the order to "Sit

125

down and shut up," and Ruin smacked the guy behind the counter.

The new guy's expression flickered from angry bewilderment to worshipful awe. He bowed his head until his forehead touched the counter. "Oh, wow. It's an honor to be in your presence. I'm not worthy of witnessing your grand acts of vengeance."

Jett shot Ruin a baleful look. "Did you infect him with a Victorian sensibility along with the admiration?"

Ruin splayed his arms, laughing. "I don't know how it works."

"The important part works like this," Nox said, planting his hands on the other side of the counter. "You're going to prove how worthy you are by telling us everything you know about the people who run the Skeleton Corps."

The guy peeked up at him as well as he could while only raising his head an inch from the counter, still in full deference mode. "I'm so sorry. I have no idea who's at the top. I'm not worthy of *them* either. Not that they hold a candle to your greatness."

Nox puffed up his massive frame a little. I didn't think he minded the effusive compliments, overly formal or not. "Fine. Then tell us about the highest people you *do* know about. Who gives you your marching orders?"

The guy's mouth twisted. "I don't know her name, but I know the place she usually operates out of. I can bring you to her if that would satisfy your request."

"Sure, sure." Nox waved at him to get moving.

"It's like a fucking scavenger hunt," Kai muttered. "Collect all the pieces, and maybe we'll get a prize at the end."

"*Someone's* got to know what the hell is going on in this city," Nox said.

Presumably someone did, but it wasn't the woman the new guy led us to. She pulled a gun on us the second we sauntered into the back room of her laundromat. Thankfully, our guy was so concerned for the well-being of his honored brainwashers that he leapt between her and us, which gave Kai the opening to wallop her into dropping the gun and kicking it away. Then he sent the guy off to take a nap on top of the dryers while Ruin socked some terror into the woman.

She started trembling from head to foot so hard I thought she might jitter right into the wall. "Please don't hurt me," she mumbled. "Whatever you want— just leave me alone."

Nox folded his arms across his chest and spoke with a tone like he'd restrained a sigh. "We want to know who's in charge of the Skeleton Corps and where we can find them."

Although she didn't know either, she hastily babbled something about a construction site where some guys who might be able to tell us were working. "And off we go again!" Kai said in a singsong voice as we headed out to the bikes.

By the time we reached the construction site, it was late enough that all the regular workers had gone home. And dark enough that I couldn't make out much more than the vague shape of some steel girders and a very large, black pit. As far as I could tell, they were constructing either an immense swimming pool or a gateway to hell.

The lights were on in the small office trailer in the corner of the lot. We all tramped over there across the uneven dirt, picking up multiple voices carrying from inside. Jett, who couldn't do much to defend the group with his artistic talents, pulled the gun out of the back of his jeans and held it ready. I glanced around for anything liquid I could make use of. I didn't feel quite ready to start flinging people's blood around yet.

But it seemed the Skeleton Corps members weren't as distracted as they appeared. Before we'd quite made it to the trailer, the door flew open, and three men charged out at us, already firing their own guns.

Nox roared and swung his hand through the air, and as far as I could tell he used his ghostly energy to literally punch one of the bullets out of the way. Kai had ducked low at the first creak of the door's hinges, dodging another, and rammed into one of the men's legs, knocking him to the ground. "Shoot your colleagues where it'll hurt but not kill them," he ordered as they fell.

The guy gave it his best, well, shot, but his aim was shaky from the fall. His bullet went wide, and then Ruin collided with the third man, heedless of the bloody streak across his upper arm where the last of the initial shots had grazed him.

That guy immediately started whimpering and

huddling in the dirt. The first guy swung around, pulling out yet another gun, but Jett fulfilled what Kai's dupe hadn't been able to and shot it right out of his hand, severing a few fingers in the process.

Nox hefted the one guy who wasn't under supernatural control up and hung him from the hook of a nearby crane truck. As the man dangled there, sputtering and cursing, a frog hopped up beside me and let out a curious croak.

"No swimming here yet," I told it. "But he sounds like he's practically speaking your language."

The second guy took aim again even though his services were no longer needed, so Kai gave him another wallop and ordered him to bring anything useful out of the office. Nox peered up at the guy he'd hooked.

"We don't really need all three, do we?" he said. "And this one's particularly annoying."

The memory of our other recent battle with a group of the Skeleton Corps guys came back to me with a prickling chill. "Wait. We should check them all for Gauntt marks."

"Right!" Ruin yanked up his victim's shirt sleeve, ignoring the dude's whimpers for mercy. "Nothing here," he announced.

Nox took a knife out of his pocket and simply sliced open the hooked guy's shirt from the collar to take a close look. He batted away the guy's flailing legs and frowned. "Damn it. This one's gotten the Gauntt treatment. I guess you'd better crack him open."

My heart sank as I stepped closer. The guy flailed

EVA CHASE

harder, even though my version of cracking open was a heck of a lot less bloody than Nox's would have been.

"Let me guess," I said to the guy. "A long time ago when you were a kid, Nolan and maybe Marie Gauntt paid you a visit or two to talk about special school programs or some crap like that."

"What the fuck are you going on about, crazy bitch?" the guy sneered, like he wasn't essentially giant fish bait at this point.

Kai's man had just dumped a heap of papers on the ground outside the office. "Check him for a mark, and then get over here and shut this asshole up," Nox ordered Kai.

The office man didn't have a mark either, so Kai gave him another smack with the orders to climb up one of the girders as fast as he could go. He waited until the guy was so high he'd have trouble getting down without making like a lemming and going splat, and then swatted the jerk dangling in front of me. "Keep your mouth shut and stay still."

Nox lowered the hook so I could grasp the guy's shoulder. He stared at me, his eyes wild with panicked rage.

"I'm just helping you remember," I told him, a little tersely because, after all, he'd tried to shoot us. Then I focused my attention on the magic emanating from the mark.

This time I was surer of what I was doing. I called up the power inside me, which was already humming from the fight, and slammed it into the barrier that walled off the horrible moments from the man's past. Once, twice, three times, harder with each impact. With the last one, I gritted my teeth and let a flare of my frustration offer an extra burst of fuel.

The Gauntts' magic shattered. The man twitched, the fury fading from his eyes. It was replaced by a haunted expression.

Kai prodded him in the gut. "Stay still but talk."

"What the fuck did you do to me?" the guy demanded at once, wriggling on the hook. "I didn't—this can't be real—"

"I didn't do anything," I said. "*They* did it. The Gauntts. Tell us what they put you through, and we can make them pay."

He gulped air and shuddered. Kai's instructions must have forced him to say *something*, but it couldn't make him answer my question exactly. "No. Fuck no. I never wanted— I told them to go away— But they still — *No*. And then out there at the marsh—"

I perked up in an instant, my mind shooting to the marsh plants we'd found decorating the bedrooms in the Gauntts' home. "What about the marsh? Did the Gauntts take you out here?"

"I'm not telling you fucking anything," the guy snarled. "This is insane. I—"

Kai gave him one last smack. "Shut up and come with us. If you don't want to tell us, you can show us."

thirteen

Lily

I couldn't see anything particularly special about the spot in the marsh that the Skeleton Corps guy had led us to last night. In the darkness, it'd had an unsettlingly creepy vibe, but all of the marsh did. It was hard for rattling reeds and groaning logs to give off a cheerful atmosphere even in full sunlight.

Which was how we were looking at them now, standing on the narrow spit where a sliver of solid ground jutted an extra twenty or so feet from the shore into the midst of the cattails, like a dock that'd sprouted out of the earth.

The rattling and the groaning blended with the softer whisper of the breeze and the gentle buzzing of nearby insect life into a song that rippled through me.

My throat constricted, but I thought about what Jett had said the other night about making art around our brokenness. Maybe I couldn't be whole enough to bring music to life without being sure of Marisol's safety. That wasn't something wrong with my creative spirit. It just showed how important she was to me.

I wished I could give Jett as easy an answer to his own pain. The thought of what he'd been through with his parents—the strain that'd come into his voice when he'd admitted he wasn't sure he could ever create the art he wanted to—still brought an ache into my stomach when I remembered it.

He looked like his usual grimly obstinate self right now, no sign that he was fretting over those issues. I guessed he'd been living with them his whole life, so that made sense.

He slung his hands in his pockets and gazed along the length of the spit. "Where are we going to place these things? We really should have Kai along for this. He'll probably come and tell us we did it all wrong anyway."

Nox strode down the stretch of grassy earth, which was hardly wide enough for two people to stand next to each other—harder when one of those people was him with his increasingly brawny frame. "Kai's busy taking care of things on the *professional* end. Fucking suits." He paused, studying the tufts of reeds and the swaying cattails on either side of the spit. "The Skeleton Corps guy said the Gauntts took him out to the end here and dunked him in the water, right?"

I nodded, my gut clenching up even more at *that* memory. When we'd reached the spit with the guy in the middle of the night, a light smack from Ruin had broken his silence. He'd babbled about his trip to the marsh with the Gauntts while a squad of frogs had hopped over to join us, stopping around him in a semi-circle like they were enthralled by his performance.

Except it hadn't been just a performance. It'd obviously really happened. Nolan and Marie Gauntt had led him out here some twenty-five years ago when he'd been nine, made him strip, and soaked him in the marsh water until he'd been shaking so hard with the chills that he'd blacked out. Lord only knew what they'd done to him after that.

"None of the other people with marks we talked to mentioned coming out here," I said. "I wonder if that was some kind of special case."

But even as I said those words, I didn't really believe them. The Gauntts had brought pieces of the marsh into their home—slept next to them. Maybe they sometimes had the kids knocked out when they brought them here. Maybe not all of the kids qualified for whatever they'd been up to at the marsh. That guy had only remembered coming here once. And we'd only broken into a few other people's memories of their abuse.

Had Nolan dragged Marisol out here, years ago or recently?

The frogs that'd gathered around my feet today ribbeted but offered no insight. I frowned down at them. "It'd be really nice if you could figure out how to talk. I bet you've seen all kinds of things."

Ruin chuckled. "They probably don't pay attention to anything except the water and the flies they want to eat. Pretty nice life, being a frog." He loped over to join Nox by the end of the spit and swiveled to take in both sides of the marsh.

This spot was farther from the town than our previous haunt near my family's home, about two miles distant from where the guys' former bodies had been dumped. There was enough of a hill to the ground in between that I couldn't see the house from here.

"The marsh must be magic!" Ruin announced abruptly. "It kept us kind-of alive, and it gave Lily powers, and the Gauntts were doing something weird with it too."

"Lots of other people come out here," I said doubtfully. "I mean, not this exact spot." There wasn't even a proper road to this end of the marsh. We'd had to trek the last mile on foot. "But all around the lake. People go swimming out in the end by the marina or out of their boats. At least some of the tap water must be filtered from it. We don't *all* have special talents."

"It doesn't matter one way or another," Nox said. "We just want to catch the Gauntts if they come out here again and find out what the hell *they* use it for."

He pulled a small black device from his pocket and fixed it into the ground at the end of the spit so it pointed toward the foot. After folding several reeds over to disguise it without blocking the sensor area, he walked back to the foot of the spit and set up another device pointing across it, giving it the same treatment.

"Will the signal reach all the way to us even when we're in Mayfield?" I asked. Before he'd left for work, Kai had chatted up some techie contacts he'd made and procured these motion sensors for us. But they didn't do us much good if we didn't know they were sensing motion.

Nox nodded. "As long as the batteries hold out—and they're supposed to be good for at least a week before we have to change them. There's some kind of a router or something they connect to that'll bounce the signal to us. I don't know. Kai talked about it like it made sense to him, but it's hard to tell with that guy. At least he thinks the woman who told *him* about it knew what she was talking about."

A couple of the frogs bounded past us, drawing my gaze. "And they won't be triggered by anything a lot smaller than a person?"

Nox's lips twitched. "I believe he asked about that factor specifically, considering your froggy fanbase."

I made a face at him, and he laughed, looping his arm around mine. "Good thing they're not your only fans, huh," he teased, leaning close enough that his breath tickled my ear.

A flush washed over me, and I swatted him. "They've been useful in their own ways."

Jett knelt down by the nearest motion detector and adjusted the angles of a few of the bent reeds. I couldn't tell whether he was simply enhancing their aesthetic appeal or improving on the camouflage.

I stepped close, and he pushed himself upright and away at the same moment, accidentally backing into me. I only stumbled for a second before he caught my arm. In that instant, we were so close that the flush I'd felt with Nox deepened into a flare of heat. When Jett was touching me, it was hard not to remember his hands on me that one early morning in bed, gripping my hair, squeezing my ass as he ground his groin against mine.

"Sorry," he muttered brusquely, and yanked himself away as if my heat had scalded him. I thought a visible shiver passed through his arm, and a lump rose in my throat.

I knew he wanted to protect me as much as the others did, but it was so hard to read where he stood other than that. Did I outright disgust some part of him? Maybe he thought it was obscene that I could want to get it on with all three of his friends and him too.

The other guys didn't seem to mind the sharing thing, but that didn't mean Jett had to agree.

I turned away and found Nox watching us with a pensive expression and a gleam flickering into his eyes. He jerked his chin toward the bikes. "Let's head out. Don't want there to be any chance of the Gauntts catching on that *we've* caught on to their special spot."

We tramped across the damp grass, the frogs following us in a hopping procession, until we reached the gravel-laced spot where the guys had parked their bikes. Nox studied his friends. "Ruin, why don't you go grab us some lunch? I'm craving the barbeque chicken from that place in Bedard."

"Perfect!" Ruin said, even though the trip would take him an hour out of his way. "They have the best spicy wings." He licked his lips, no doubt imagining sauce so hot it'd incinerate anyone else's tongue, and shot off on his bike.

Nox motioned to Jett next, unhooking the strap of the spare helmet from his handlebars and slinging it onto Jett's. "You take Lily. I have something quick to take care of that I don't want her along for."

"What?" Jett said, startled, but he didn't have time to argue about it. Nox swung his leg over his bike and was roaring off an instant later.

The artist glanced at me, swiping his hand across his mouth. "Well, I guess we'd better get going."

He climbed onto his motorcycle. I pulled on my helmet and positioned myself gingerly behind him. There wasn't much room on the seat for two, but the thought of pressing myself right against him like I would have with Nox, breasts to back and core to ass, made my nerves skitter. I didn't like the idea of Jett feeling awful the whole way back to the apartment.

"Get right on," he said gruffly, revving the engine. "I don't want you to fall off. That helmet won't do much for the rest of you."

At his insistence, I tucked myself a little closer, sliding my arms around his waist. Jett shifted on the seat as if to confirm I was secure and then took off down the potholed lane.

I kept my butt just a little farther back than I would have with Nox so there was a tiny gap between us in the most intimate region, but that meant I had to lean into Jett's back to keep my balance. I tipped my head to one side against the worn leather of his jacket and closed my eyes.

It was easier not to worry about anything when I was focusing on the fast yet steady thumping of his heart beneath my ear and the growl of the engine.

Through the smell of the leather, I could pick up whiffs that were distinctly Jett: a sharp note of paint, which he probably had a smudge of on him somewhere, and a hint of the cola he chugged so much of I wouldn't be surprised if it started coming out of his pores. The scent was so perfectly him that another pang shot through me, a mix of affection and regret.

He kept so much to himself that I wasn't sure I knew him anywhere near as well as I did the others, but I cared about him all the same. He'd been here for me, protected me when I needed it, talked me through my doubts even though talking didn't come naturally to him.

I wished I knew how to stop the uncomfortable vibe that developed between us so often.

It turned out that Nox had been thinking about that vibe too. We pulled up at the apartment next to his bike, which was already in the lot. It must have been a short errand—if he'd actually gone on one at all and not used that as an excuse to stick me with Jett. When we got upstairs, we found the Skullbreakers boss in the living room, anticipation radiating off him concretely enough that my skin quivered with it.

"All right," he said, all commanding authority. "Come with me."

He ushered us into the guys' bedroom. The Murphy bed was still lowered from the night before. A condom packet sat on the bedside table. Jett halted just over the threshold, stiffening a bit at the sight of it.

"What's going on?" he asked.

Nox set his hands on my shoulders from behind and then trailed them down to my waist, where he fingered the hem of my shirt. He gazed past me at Jett. "You want her. It's obvious to anyone who has freaking eyes. It's probably obvious to you too, so I don't know why you're insisting on holding yourself back."

A reddish tinge colored Jett's cheeks. "Just because I don't want to—"

"You fucking *do*," Nox interrupted, his tone getting firmer. "You practically fuck her with your eyes at least ten times a day. So I think it's about time you put yourself and her and all of us out of our misery and did the deed properly."

The heat that unfurled low in my belly wasn't entirely comfortable. "Nox," I started.

But Jett put to words my exact objection. "Are you seriously ordering me to have sex with Lily?"

"I'm ordering you to pull your head out of your ass and get out of your own way," Nox said. He grazed his fingertips over my waist beneath my shirt. "You want him too, don't you, Siren?"

My pulse stuttered. I wasn't going to lie. "I do," I said, a blush flaring in my cheeks. "But not if he isn't into it. I don't want Jett to force himself."

Nox snorted. "He's forcing himself *not* to touch you." He tugged at my shirt, and I raised my arms instinctively so he could peel it off. After dropping it on the floor, he brought his hands to my breasts, cupping them through my bra, and glanced at Jett again. "Tell me I'm wrong. Tell me it's not taking everything in you not to walk over here and worship our woman."

Jett's eyes blazed over my skin, and for a second I thought Nox was right. But he said in a taut voice, "Just because some part of me likes the idea doesn't mean it's a good one."

"What could possibly be wrong with it?" Nox demanded. "Give me one good reason why it's better for you to be driven to distraction by all the things you're not letting yourself have instead of just having them."

"She already has all of you," Jett shot back, more forcefully than he usually spoke. "Maybe I want something different with her. Does that bother *you* so much?"

Nox only raised his eyebrows. "Just because you get busy with her doesn't mean it'd be the same. Give us a little credit." He nuzzled the side of my face with a flick of his tongue along the back of my ear. His thumbs dipped inside my bra to roll my nipples, and the sparks of pleasure made me gasp even though I was trying to focus on Jett. "Is it the same with the three of us, Minnow? Do I fuck you like Ruin does? Or like Kai?"

The thought was so absurd I almost laughed. "No," I said. "You're all different. Very different." But still oh so good. Just remembering how they'd all worked me over together the other day in their various ways had me soaking my panties despite myself.

"That's right," Nox said in the same low tone he used when he called me "good girl." "You're not giving her something better by holding back, Jett. You're just denying her whatever it is that only you could give her. And denying yourself too."

Jett still just stood there, though he couldn't seem to tear his eyes away from Nox's hands on my chest. When he finally yanked his gaze back to my face and then to Nox, his voice came out ragged. "You don't know that."

"I do," Nox insisted. "That's why I call the shots. You don't feel right deciding to go for it? Fine. I'm taking that decision out of your hands. Fuck her in your own special Jett way. Make her scream until the people downstairs wonder why the hell they don't have it that good. You want it to be art? Make *her* art." Letting go of me, he grabbed a few of the paint cans off the dresser and set them on the bed.

Jett's gaze followed the movement, and his tongue darted out to wet his lips. A little of the tension in his expression faded, his eyes lighting up. A fresh quiver of heat raced through my veins.

Was that all there was to it? He needed to frame the act in the right way, to see it as more than just mindless hooking up? It would always have meant more than that to me, but maybe that hadn't been obvious.

He should know now that I was definitely a willing participant in Nox's suggestion. I reached behind me to unclasp my bra and let it fall to my feet. Then I shucked off shoes, pants, and panties, until I stood naked before the two of them. Ignoring the twinge of self-consciousness that tickled over my skin, I climbed onto the bed.

"It'd be an honor to be your canvas," I said softly.

Jett let out a low sound in his throat. He glanced at Nox as if he needed final confirmation that his boss really was not just approving this but urging him on. At Nox's motion, he moved to the edge of the bed. His gaze remained fixed on me now.

"Are you sure?" he said, the words coming out raw. "It'll probably be a mess."

I grinned wholeheartedly. "I've seen what you can do. Even if it is, it'll be a beautiful mess."

He eased over so he was sitting right next to me. His hand hovered over my shoulder, and for a second I thought he was going to kiss me. Then he grasped one of the paint cans instead. Once he'd opened it, he dipped his fingers inside. They came out dripping with a deep midnight blue.

Jett traced the first line along my jaw and down my throat. He flicked his thumb over my chin, and something in his eyes shifted. He tugged my face toward him and finally captured my mouth.

As our lips melded together, his fingers kept

sweeping over my body, shadowing my collarbone and my sternum with blue, daring to dip under one breast. He broke from the kiss to grab another can, this one vibrant crimson, and streaked that over the curve of my shoulder and down my arm. Then he swiveled it around my breast, stopping just shy of the peak. A faint rasp had come into his breath as if he was having trouble keeping it stable.

My own breaths were quickening. I was dying to kiss him again, to lean into his touch, but I didn't want to take away the control he'd claimed over the situation, that had made this encounter feel right to him. So I kept my hands braced against the covers, even as I felt my arousal pooling between my legs.

Jett dabbed purple across my nipples, drawing a gasp from my throat at the contact. He paused, swirling the hue so it mingled with the red farther down, swiveling his thumb over the peaks again and again until they were harder than I'd ever thought was possible. A needy whimper tumbled from my lips.

Jett leaned in to kiss me again, a little harder and wilder this time. The fly of his jeans protruded with an unmistakable bulge. The urge to touch him swelled inside me sharper than before.

I let myself reach toward his shirt. "Can I—can I paint you too?"

Jett drew back and stared at me for a moment like it'd never occurred to him that I might ask that. He inhaled shakily, and his pupils dilated. "Yeah. Yes. Please."

I pulled off his shirt, doing my best not to let the sleeves get smeared with the paint on his multi-colored fingers. It was the first time I'd seen close up how much his spirit had filled out the once-scrawny body that used to belong to Vincent Barnes. He wasn't anywhere near as burly as Nox, but compact muscles lined his chest and abdomen. I swept my bare fingers over the taut ridges before remembering I was meant to be doing more than touching them.

I stretched my arm to find one of the pots of paint and caught some on my fingers. As I traced the blue lines down the front of Jett's chest, his breath hitched. For a minute, he didn't touch me other than resting his hands lightly on the sides of my waist, just watching me swirl and streak the colorful lines across his shoulders and neck, down to his abdomen, and back up to circle his nipples.

A faint groan reverberated through his chest. Then he was on me again, kissing me fiercely and trailing more paint across my torso.

He outlined my ribs with green and circled my belly button with purple. When he reached my hips, he dragged thick lines of red from my ass cheeks to the front of my thighs. I traced the same color across his cheeks and yanked him back in for another kiss.

I'd almost forgotten Nox was in the room. Possibly Jett had too. The Skullbreakers' leader cleared his throat softly where he was now leaning against the doorframe.

"Damn," he said. "That's fucking art all right." His hand splayed against the crotch of his jeans, where a bulge of his own was straining. "Do you mind if I fully enjoy the view, Jett?"

The implications of his question were clear, but there was so much respect in the fact that he'd asked permission at all after the orders he'd laid down earlier that I choked up a bit. The guys were devoted to me, but they had each others' backs just as much.

Jett didn't bother to drag his avid gaze away from me. "As long as Lil doesn't mind, it's fine by me. Art is meant to be appreciated."

The old nickname, soft with affection, made my heart swell with matching emotion. "I don't mind," I said, and pulled Jett back to me.

The whorls and lines that marked our bodies blurred together as we collided more eagerly. I tugged at Jett's jeans, and he peeled them off between increasingly urgent kisses. I caught the rasp of Nox's jeans unzipping and the rustling rhythm of him stroking himself as he watched, and that only made the fire of need inside me burn hotter.

Jett stroked swaths of blue down my thighs and buried his face between my legs. His tongue swiped over me like he was drawing me to life with that too, whirling over my clit and curling inside my opening, leaving me panting with the rush of bliss. My fingers dug into his hair, trailing streaks of red and blue amid the already unnaturally purple strands. As a moan slipped out of me, Nox echoed it with a groan from across the room.

Jett hummed against me almost desperately, having

his way with my sex until I was trembling on the verge of release. Through the quivers of delight that shook my body, I managed to find my voice. "Please. Inside me."

Jett let out a groan of his own and surged up over me. He snatched the condom off the table and rolled it over himself in two seconds flat. But as he lowered his hips so his erection rubbed against my clit, he paused and peered down at us.

Paint was smeared over every inch of our chests in a jumble of colors that bled into each other. "It is a bit of a mess," I said, sliding my finger through the colors on his shoulder.

"Yeah." Jett caught my eyes. Some inner turmoil churned and then faded in his dark brown eyes. "But you were right. It's a beautiful mess. *My* beautiful mess."

I lifted my hand to his cheek. "*Ours*," I said.

A rough sound escaped him. He dove in to reclaim my lips as his shaft plunged inside me.

I gasped and moaned into Jett's mouth. He set a fast pace, bucking against me, and I was already so close from the magic his tongue had worked on me earlier. The slick slide of our paint-streaked bodies made our collision feel twice as intense.

I raised my legs on either side of his hips, urging him deeper. Jett groaned and plowed into me even faster than before. With each stroke, I careened higher and higher—until I burst like a firework, splintering into light and color at some distant peak that left me shaking and breathless.

My fingers dug into his back, and my thighs

clamped around his hips. Jett dropped his head to nip the crook of my neck, heedless of the paint there. He dug his teeth in a little harder, and I came again, a fresh blaze of ecstasy right on the heels of the first. With a shudder and a hot wash of breath over my neck, Jett followed me.

He tumbled onto the covers next to me, keeping one arm around my waist. We gazed at each other, at the beautiful mess we'd made together, and a giggle bubbled out of me. Jett offered a rare smile.

"That was—" he started to say.

At the same moment, the door to the apartment crashed open.

fourteen

Lily

Jett and I sprang off the bed as if we'd been zapped. Nox had already been tucking himself back inside his jeans. He whipped around as a horde of at least ten guys charged into the living room. They were all wearing ski masks printed to look like skeleton heads.

The intruders skidded to a halt at the sight of us, freezing up momentarily as they took in Jett and me in our naked, paint-drenched glory. It wasn't how I'd have wanted to make a first impression, but the shock our appearance provoked worked in our favor.

"What the *fuck?*" one of the intruders said, and in their momentary hesitation, Nox was already hurtling into the fray.

The leader of the Skullbreakers didn't have the same problem with only being able to target one or two people at a time like Kai's and Ruin's powers. The bursts of supernatural energy that flowed out from his body with each strike did their damage regardless of how many opponents he went on to pummel next.

He blasted through the onslaught with his fists, knees, and feet flying in one direction and another, even ramming his head toward a guy a few feet away who promptly crashed into the wall as if he'd been hit by a battering ram. The crackling sound of each strike electrified the air.

The Skeleton Corps men—because who else would be in that skeletal get-up?—careened this way and that, bruises and bloody noses appearing as if out of thin air. But there were too many of them for Nox to totally subdue more than a few of them. As more figures barged into the living room, the attackers swarmed in around him, only a couple of them knocked to the floor in a daze.

Jett leapt for his gun, which was lost somewhere in the tangle of his discarded jeans. Too panicked at the sight of all those skeleton faces converging on Nox to care that I was butt naked, I dashed into the room and reached the frantic hum reverberating through me toward the nearest sources of liquid.

Water gushed from the kitchen faucet and whipped through the doorway to smack this guy and that in the face. I couldn't hit them hard enough to knock them out, but from the grunts and pawing at their eyes, I'd hurt them, maybe even messed up their vision. I sent another flood gushing over the wooden floors, making them slip and stumble on the suddenly wet surface. It splashed against my legs, licking off streaks of paint to unfurl through the currents.

Jett charged out beside me, still just as naked but ferally terrifying with his purple hair spiking every which way, his eyes blazing with anger, and his body mottled with vibrant streaks and swirls that now passed for war paint. I sure as hell wouldn't have wanted to face off with him, no matter how well-clothed I was. He pointed his gun and picked off three of the attackers in quick succession, aiming at those closest to him and farthest from Nox.

Unfortunately, several of the attackers still managed to crash into the Skullbreakers' boss. As they tackled him to the floor, he lashed out with all his limbs, catching one in the gut, another in the jaw. They reeled backward, but those he hadn't managed to strike whipped out knives and guns of their own.

"You've got some explaining to do," one of them snarled, which gave me at least a little hope that they weren't looking to kill Nox *immediately*, although they definitely didn't appear to have any qualms about doing plenty of damage in the meantime. I'd prefer he kept all his body parts attached to said body.

With a yank of my powers, I managed to fling a few cans of pop across the room from the kitchen counter. They smacked into the skulls of a few of the guys hard enough for the thin metal to burst, showering them with sticky soda as well.

Jett got off a few more shots, but he had to be careful not to hit his friend. One bullet lodged in a guy's shoulder, another in one's ass. Then three of them threw themselves at Jett, smashing the pistol from his hand and tackling him to the ground too.

Right at that moment, Ruin walked in through the open door, laden with enough takeout to feed an army. Unfortunately, he hadn't brought an army with him.

"What's all the racket?" he asked cheerfully as he crossed the threshold. "Did you start a party without—"

To give him credit, he didn't stop to gape at the chaos he found himself staring at. He dropped the bags and launched himself right into the fray in mid-sentence.

For a minute, it seemed like Ruin's arrival might turn the tide in our favor. He walloped one guy and then another, tossing one off Nox and toppling one who was about to shoot Jett in the forehead. His emotional impact bounced through the crowd, the skeleton-masked opponents flying into sudden rages at their colleagues and then faltering when he'd punched too many other jerkwads. The chaos in the room took on an air of confusion.

Nox managed to heave himself back to his feet. Jett slapped his hand into one of his opponent's faces and proved that he could alter shape as well as color. The guy's nose bulged beneath his mask, so big it obscured his vision. Jett snickered and socked him in it hard enough to send a spurt of blood from the nostrils.

One of the Skeleton Corps dickheads must have decided I'd make a good hostage by virtue of being female—and maybe being naked had something to do with it too—because he lunged at me instead of the guys. I yanked up one of the pop cans and brained him across the head with it as hard as I could. He reeled to the side, and Jett recovered his gun soon enough to shoot the jackass in the heart.

But then five more masked men barreled into the room, and suddenly we were doubly outnumbered again even with the many enemies who'd fallen. Nox swore and whipped out his fists again. Jett pulled the trigger on his pistol—and it only let out a hollow clicking that spoke of an empty chamber. Ruin rammed into two of the newcomers only to be tripped by a third so he sprawled flat on his face.

As some of the men closed in around Jett and Nox, two fell on Ruin, one jabbing down with a knife. A shriek of protest left my lips, and I lashed out with my power before I'd totally thought through what I was doing.

I had to stop him. I had to stop him *fast,* or Ruin would die.

With that certainty, all of my attention condensed on the pumping of blood through the man's veins, clenching it with an iron fist of supernatural energy. The man stiffened and shuddered, his arm veering wide. I felt down to the core of my own being the way his heart strained and the rest of his body protested at the sudden obstruction.

My own heart thudded on in a rhythm suited for a funeral possession. I could ensure this man's imminent funeral right now. All I had to do was burst apart his heart like Kai had suggested.

A trickle of nausea wrapped around my stomach. I didn't *want* to be a killer. But if I didn't do this thing, then the asswipe would just go back to killing Ruin. For the second time.

If I was in this thing, if I was going to stand with my men, I had to go all in.

The decision darted through my mind in the space of a few heartbeats, and then I wrenched at the blood contained in the man's body like I was hauling on one end of a tug-of-war rope that would determine the fate of the universe.

Blood crashed into the man's heart in a violent punch. The impact of the shattering muscles echoed through my awareness. Then the douchebag was crumpling over, a streak of blood dribbling from the corner of his mouth.

I'd done it. I felt sick but also invincible. Ruin caught my gaze as he yanked himself out from beneath the guy and shot me a brilliant smile that made it all seem okay.

He whacked the calf of the other Corps man near him, who immediately barreled at his companions who were surrounding Nox. In the ensuing scuffle, Nox requisitioned one of the attacker's knives and did a little creative carving that left them all slumped in a pile. Ruin had rushed to help Jett next, and the two of them batted around the last few Skeleton Corps members like cats with wounded mice.

"Wait!" I said quickly before they could deal out the final fatal blows. "One of them might know something useful about the people in charge."

Jett grunted in approval and shoved one of the guys backward. Nox caught him, whirled him around, kicked his feet out from under him, and pinned him to the ground. Ruin rammed his hands out in a double punch, catching both of the other remaining dipshits in the stomach. They both crumpled, cringing with both pain and fear.

"No more," one of them started babbling. "You people are demons."

"Not quite," Nox said from his human perch, sounding amused.

"Now you tell us what you know about the people who told you to attack us," Ruin declared with apparent glee.

One of the men tipped over on his side and just rocked to and fro on the floor, sucking his thumb. The other trembled from head to toe.

"I can't," he whined. "If they find out—they'll hang my guts from a flagpole."

Nox cocked his head like he was thinking that might not be a bad tactic and then flashed his teeth. "What do you think *we're* going to do to you if you don't talk?"

The guy shuddered again. "You don't know what they're like. Please don't punish me. Just let me go. Or kill me. Whatever. I can't do this." His voice was rising into a wail.

Jett snorted. "I think you hit them a little too hard, Ruin."

Ruin looked down at his fists. "I don't know how to un-punch them."

An idea came to me, perfect and terrible at the same time. I raised my chin and forced the words from my mouth. "Maybe we need to show him just how bad things can get with us. We can do a lot more than just kill him. We can tear him apart from the inside out."

I raised my hand, and Nox's eyes gleamed with approval. He nodded and aimed another vicious look at our former attacker. "And Lily's the nicest out of all of us. Consider this a preview."

Somehow it was easier this time—maybe because I knew I might not have to kill him. Maybe because I *had* killed someone already, and the world hadn't fallen in on me. I summoned the hum inside me, tapping my fingers against my hip so the rhythm would give me better control, and reached toward the fluid flowing through the man's veins.

It wasn't hard at all. If anything, it was horrifyingly easy. I pushed and pulled at his bloodstream, making one vein swell and another deflate and battering his heart with little jabbing spurts. The man jerked with those assaults, his face going sallow, and guilt coiled around my stomach. But I didn't let myself stop.

He needed to tell us what he knew. We needed to end this war before the Skeleton Corps destroyed my men all over again.

"What are you doing?" he asked in a quavering voice, and gulped with an agonized sound when I prodded him again. His mouth twisted at a queasy angle. He pressed his hand to his chest.

"She can keep doing this to you, and she can do it to every one of your friends," Nox said darkly. "And this is her going easy. Do you want to find out just *how* bad it can get when someone's playing with your blood right inside your body?"

A sharper tremor ran through the man's frame, and his mouth burst open. "All right! All right! Please stop. No more. I—I'll tell you about my bosses."

fifteen

Nox

I looked across the street at the building and scoffed in disbelief. "*This* is what the big bad Skeleton Corps have been operating out of?"

"For the time being," Kai said, ever the pedant, with a nudge of his glasses up his nose. "The one guy before did tell us that they move their base of operations around a lot."

Ruin chuckled. "Hey, who doesn't like ice cream?"

He might have had a point there, but the ice cream parlor across from us still didn't have the imposing grandeur I'd been expecting from the home base of the Skeleton Corps's upper echelon. It was painted in pastel colors. The sign had a cute little kitten licking an ice cream cone. I'd be willing to bet a thousand dollars that the door let out a cheerful jingle when anyone opened it.

"Maybe the dope didn't know what he was taking about," Jett said with a similarly skeptical expression. "Or maybe he was still terrified enough of *them* to lie to us."

"Or maybe it'd make sense for them to use a place like this," Lily put in. "If no one would expect a gang to operate out of it, then no one's going to be coming around hassling them."

"And also," Ruin said, "free ice cream." From the gleam in his eyes, he was planning on scooping a bunch for himself once we got in there.

Lily rolled her eyes at him with obvious affection. "Yes, that is a benefit too."

I shifted my weight on my feet. I still didn't really *like* having her along for a confrontation like this. I'd have preferred for there to be several miles and multiple steel barriers between her and the menaces who'd slaughtered us two decades ago—and tried to murder us at least a few more times since I'd returned. But there was no denying that she'd held her own during the attack yesterday. The Skeleton Corps invaders might have *succeeded* in murdering us if she hadn't stepped in with the new bloody dimension to her powers.

And when I'd suggested that she let us handle this on our own, she'd refused before I'd even gotten all the words out. *Your fight with them is mine too, just like you wouldn't leave me alone to tackle the Gauntts. You said I'm part of the Skullbreakers now, didn't you?*

I couldn't argue with that. And it was her fight for all sorts of other reasons now too. Not least of which being the fact that it was her apartment we'd spent several hours cleaning bodies and blood out of last night.

There were still a few purple streaks in her hair by the nape of her neck, where she hadn't managed to wash out the final traces of paint from more enjoyable activities earlier that night. Even with the battle ahead of us, the sight made my cock twitch.

I'd never have said I was any kind of art aficionado, but the picture she and Jett had made yesterday? I'd call that a fucking masterpiece.

Jett cracked his knuckles. "So, strange place or not, are we sticking to the plan?"

I didn't figure we were in a good position to stand around here coming up with a new one, right across the street from our targets. I glanced at Kai, since the whole advance preparation thing was more his specialty anyway. He nodded.

"It may work even better in there than the kind of setting we'd have pictured. Less room for them to maneuver. We just need to make sure we keep our individual targets separate. If we double up, we'll only be half as effective."

I might have dropped out of high school, but I could follow that much math. I nodded and motioned to the others. "Let's teach them a thing or two about messing with the Skullbreakers."

"Don't break *all* of their skulls," Kai reminded us.

"We don't know yet who offed us. It could be old-timers who aren't as active anymore. But someone in there should know."

He and Jett took out their guns. I left mine in the back of my jeans since my fists were better weapons with their new supernaturally enhanced punch, and we charged across the street toward the parlor.

It was technically open, but the Skeleton Corps didn't appear to have been doing much to drum up business in however long it'd been since they'd taken the shop over. When we burst inside, there was no one in the building but several men who looked to be coming up on middle-aged, sitting around two of the little formica tables pushed together into one long one. A dude in the middle of the bunch was eating a fucking sundae.

The lights gleamed down on them, the polished tabletops, and the glass display case on the left side that held the spread of ice cream tubs. A sweet, creamy smell hung in the air, making the violence we were about to commit feel momentarily absurd. But they'd chosen this venue, not us.

"Are you the Skeleton Corps?" I demanded as the men jumped up. I'd have preferred to skip the introductions, but we weren't sure exactly how accurate the squealer's information was. It wouldn't do us much good if we killed the wrong gang leaders and ended up with some other syndicate out for revenge on *us*.

The guy nearest us snarled and lunged, which was

enough of an answer. If it'd been a simple misunderstanding, they could have just said so.

They *all* sprang up and rushed at us, guns and knives whipping out in a jumble of motion. We focused on the figures at the front of the pack.

Kai and Ruin leapt in first, as we'd planned. Kai socked the first guy in the jaw, ordering him to "Shield us from your friends and hit them back," at the same time. Ruin kneed another prick in the gut.

I hadn't been sure if he'd actually been able to follow through on the emotional programming we'd discussed, considering he didn't always seem fully in control of how it turned out, but the guy immediately spun around to face his colleagues with a yodeling sort of battle cry.

"Death to anyone who challenges the kings of the city," he bellowed.

The fact that he obviously meant us and not the men he'd been standing with seconds ago threw his friends for a loop. They wavered for a second in the middle of their charge. In that second, the first guy punched one hard enough to break his nose and the second headbutted another in the gut.

The other guys hollered for help, and a few underlings came hustling out of a door at the back of the room. But it was nothing like their attack on us last night. They must have felt pretty confident in their secrecy and their ability to defend themselves here. They'd been counting on the horde they'd sent after us to bring us down.

Tough luck.

The two men Ruin and Kai had supernaturally conscripted to our cause formed a buffer between us at the rest of the Skeleton dudes. They swung and slashed at anyone who tried to get by them. With so many still on the other side, a couple dodged past, but Ruin caught one of them with a jab that had him flailing and wailing like he'd been sent into a living nightmare.

Jett caught the other asshole and tossed him over the glass counter. I barged around it just as the jerk staggered to his feet and slammed his head into one of the ice-cream buckets. How was that for a brain freeze?

From the corner of my eye, I could see Lily working her own brand of magic. There'd been a bottle of vodka on the table, open for pouring into the scattered glasses, but she'd emptied it in an instant. The globs of alcohol soared through the air and seared into one guy's and another's eyes in quick succession. When she ran out of that, a spurt of blood spewed from the dude's broken nose and splashed another guy in the face, temporarily blinding him.

She could do way worse damage if she wanted to. The thought of how she'd conquered those imbeciles last night got me hard all over again. But it was only good if she was in the zone and loving it too. I didn't want her to push herself past the limits of her strength or her conscience.

Another guy came tearing around the display case toward me. Energy crackled through my arms, and I heaved him onto the tubs without even touching him. Now he was freezing his ass off.

I sure hoped whoever did the actual work around here knew better than to serve that stuff tomorrow.

The bosses of the Skeleton Corps were smart enough to know when they were beaten—and to realize that there wasn't any point in committing suicide via idiocy. The three of the seven still standing dashed for the back door. I motioned to Jett, and we sprinted after them. He shot at the escapees and caught one of them in the heel, sending him tumbling.

Just as the first of the bunch reached the doorway, still several feet ahead of us, his body jerked. His hand slammed into the doorframe, and he clutched at it as he pressed his other palm to his chest. Over his heart.

My gaze shot to Lily. She was staring at him from the other side of the room, one of her hands balled tight at her side, the other drumming some kind of rhythm on her thigh. Her hair lifted off her shoulders as if an electrical storm was whipping through it. A heady quiver raced over my skin.

She was some fucking woman, all right.

The guy she was targeting had blocked the doorway well enough that Jett caught up with the dude right behind him. He hurled that guy toward one of the tables, where Ruin fell on him like the Corps dude was some kind of banquet—except using his fists rather than his teeth, thank the Devil. With a one-two punch, Ruin had the prick curled up and whimpering for mercy.

The first guy Ruin had afflicted with his chosen emotions, the one who'd been battling valiantly for our side, snapped out of it. But his brother-at-arms under Kai's spell had been knocked out in the brawl, so Kai stepped up without hesitation and cracked the other jerk across the head with his knuckles. "Stand still and keep quiet."

The guy stiffened. The man in the doorway slowly turned, his hand still pressed to his chest, his face haggard. He swayed on his feet.

"What is this about?" he rasped. "Who the hell are you, and what the fuck do you want with us?"

Finally, someone was asking the important questions. I tipped my head to Lily, and her jaw worked as she must have eased off on the guy just a little. Jett dragged up the man whose foot he'd shot and smacked him down in one of the chairs, using his tie to attach him to the back of it like a noose. My artist friend held his gun at the ready in case he needed to blast the other foot to smithereens.

All of the underlings were lying dazed and useless. Of the seven top dogs we'd interrupted, one was gone from this world, one was temporarily dead to it, one was under Kai's control, and two were having nervous breakdowns thanks to Ruin. The heel-less prick and Mr. Heart Attack were the only ones in their right minds and conscious.

If I could add up those odds, I was pretty sure they could too. And you didn't get to the top by being willing to sacrifice yourself on principle. You got there by making whatever compromises you needed to in order to survive.

I stepped closer, folding my arms over my chest and staring down the bastard by the doorway. "You don't need to know anything about who we are except that we're no one you want to mess with. But hopefully our demonstration today has proven that well enough, since how we've dealt with your lowlifes didn't get through to you. We're not anything you're used to dealing with, and so you can either *make* a deal with us, or you can die too."

The Skeleton Corps guy wet his lips. "Then I'll ask again—what do you want?"

I raised my hand and popped up my forefinger. "First, no more attacks on me or anyone who stands with me. You back off on us, and we won't have to arrange another 'meeting' like this. We're not looking to take over your stomping grounds. All we ever wanted was some answers."

Well, and the appropriate compensation for those answers, but I wasn't going to mention that.

"Answers to what?" the guy snapped.

I tipped my head to Kai. It always looked better if it was clear more than one of you knew how to do more than swing your fists around.

The brainiac moved forward, his face flushed from the exertion of the fight. "Twenty-one years ago, a gang called the Skullbreakers was operating out of a hangout near Lovell Rise. A bunch of Skeleton Corps guys crashed the building and killed the leaders. Presumably at least one of you still knows who instigated that attack and who participated in it?"

"What does any of that matter to you?" the man demanded.

He was getting more spirit back than I liked. I motioned to Lily with an encouraging smile, and the drumming of her fingers sped up again. The man twitched, his hand slapping back against his chest.

"It's none of your business *why* we want to know," I informed him. "Cough up the answers, or we'll toss you aside and find someone else who's willing to give them."

The asshole's voice came out strangled. "I only know bits and pieces about it," he muttered. "I was new then, and no one talks about it much anymore. Branson was there." He nodded to the unconscious dude who'd previously been Kai's puppet. "I think McCallum and Perrucci gave the orders. McCallum's dead, and Perrucci is retired now."

An idea took root in my mind. We could have shot Branson right now and demanded to be directed to Perrucci... but that seemed like letting them off easy. I wanted all of them to face up to what they'd done with maximum torment. They had twenty-one years of payback coming to them.

"Sorry to hear about McCallum," I said casually. "But we'll have to get the rest of that bunch together. It was quite an event, and we'd like to celebrate it."

The man blinked, puzzlement crossing his face. "I guess that might be arranged."

Ruin let out a whoop. "Party time!"

I snapped my fingers. "There you go. That's our last condition—the condition of us not coming back and exploding your heart inside your chest or getting you to carve it out yourself because we said so. A reunion of the Skullbreakers' destroyers so we can properly repay them for all they've done."

Jett grinned, maybe a little too fiercely to pass as friendly. The man's eyes darted between us. But it must have been clear that saying "No" would be a death sentence.

He cleared his throat. "All right. It might take a little while to track down everyone involved, if you really want all of them."

"All of them still living," I said with a smile. "It wouldn't be fair to leave a single one of them out."

sixteen

Lily

I leaned my elbows onto the table and watched Nox as he paced by the apartment's living room windows, talking to Ruin with ample enthusiasm. They were working out the details of their big "party" where they'd "thank" the guys who'd had a hand in killing them for the blood they'd shed.

It was nice seeing them in such a good mood. They'd waited more than two decades for this revenge. But their good spirits only cast my own low ones into sharper relief.

"Do you think they'll recognize us?" Ruin asked, grinning at the thought.

Nox hummed to himself. "I doubt it. We don't look exactly like our old selves, and they haven't seen us in more than twenty years. Who knows how good a look they got at us when they were blasting us to bits anyway? We'd never dealt with the Skeleton Corps before. It sounds like they only came after us because of those Silver Scythe pricks talking shit."

"And they'd hardly be expecting to encounter the men they murdered twenty-one years ago to turn up both alive and unaged," Kai put in as he sat down next to me, bringing the laptop he'd bought—or, well, more likely stolen, knowing these guys—for himself. "The mind tends to reject evidence that contradicts what it believes to be possible. At best, they might wonder if we're direct descendants."

Ruin clapped his hands. "The sons of the fallen gangsters come back for revenge. I like that story too."

Nox snorted. "We'll try out both if we ever make it into a stage play. But we have to make sure we get all of the bastards who pitched in and are still around together. As soon as we take down some, anyone who isn't there will know to run."

Jett came over to make some suggestions of how he might use his powers to subtly manipulate the party décor in ways that would hinder any escape attempts—or provide additional avenues for torment—and Kai turned to me. "Your hashtag has accumulated quite a few submissions. I figured it was time we went through to check for the local videos and see if there's anyone around with marks we could break. Get a better idea of the Gauntts' preferred demographics too."

"Sure," I said, sitting up straighter in my chair. I was

eager to get going with some kind of constructive planning myself. If I sat too long with my thoughts, the memories of wrenching at the Skeleton Corps guys' blood trickled up through my mind, especially the moment when I'd blasted apart the one man's heart. The echo of that sensation sent a clammy feeling over my skin even as my pulse thumped harder with a spurt of adrenaline.

I was powerful. I was a force to be reckoned with. But I couldn't say I loved the lengths I needed to go to with that power.

Kai tapped away on the keyboard. It was kind of amusing watching him glance at the letters, searching and pecking. He might be the brains of the Skullbreakers, but he obviously hadn't been any kind of computer expert way back when.

He frowned at the screen, jabbed at the touchpad, typed a little more, jabbed a little more. Then he sat back in his chair with his brow furrowed. "I don't like this."

My stomach twisted. "What?" I asked, leaning closer.

"They're just... gone." He clicked from one set of search results to another. When he copied a URL into the address bar, it came up with a Video Not Found page. "Computers," he muttered. "Someone broke the whole website."

My spirits were sinking fast. "I don't think so," I said. "The other videos are still working, aren't they? Search for something else."

Seemingly at random, he typed in "frog parade." Maybe he thought that wouldn't turn up much anyway. Instead, we got a long list of videos, everything from an actual parade of animated frogs to a singing Kermit to a statue of a frog at some shrine in Japan that was so big it'd have towered over me. I kind of wanted to bring my little amphibious friends across the ocean to see how well they were worshipped.

Unfortunately, as delightful as the results were, they appeared to confirm my suspicions. "The website isn't broken," I said. "Someone took down the video."

"*All* of them?" Kai said. "There were thousands yesterday. When I search for the hashtag or other keywords, nothing comes up. They were hardly salacious. Why would—" He stopped abruptly, not needing to finish the question to arrive at the answer. "The Gauntts."

Nox's head jerked toward us at the name. "What have they done now?" he growled.

"They had my sweater challenge video and all the videos responding deleted," I said. I had no trouble at all picturing Nolan and Marie coming up with some imaginary copyright infringement claim or similar to destroy the whole campaign with a snap of their fingers. "So we can't use them to look for other people they've marked."

"We don't need to," Ruin said. "We've already found a bunch—we found out about their special marsh place! We're still going to crush them."

But this was one more reminder of just how much

power the Gauntts could wield—powers totally different from what we were working with, on a playing field we couldn't even reach.

I rubbed my forehead, and Jett came up behind me. His touch was still tentative, but there was a relief in seeing that he was comfortable resting his hand on my shoulder and offering a gentle squeeze at all, rather than keeping his distance. The understanding we'd found in each other the other night hadn't been temporary.

"We are," he said, expanding on Ruin's point. "We'll crush them into very small pieces, and then we'll piss on those."

As inspiring as that imagery was, it didn't do much to reassure me right now. I lifted my head. "We still haven't found anything that can lead us to Marisol. I want to try searching with that blood harmony strategy again. I should be rested enough. And going out at night means less chance of the Gauntts spotting me however they did before." I paused. "If one of you can drive me around on your bike, that'd be great, but if you all need to be focused on the Skeleton Corps situation, I could take my car—"

Kai was already shaking his head and standing up. "I'll take you. I've already given these numbskulls my opinions anyway." He flashed a smile at his friends to show the insult was meant affectionately. "It's my fault I didn't save the videos some way the Gauntts couldn't touch them."

"You're not exactly used to internet culture," I told him. "*I* should have thought of it."

"You shouldn't go on your own anyway," Nox said, shifting on his feet like he was preparing to insist he be the one to take me for that ride.

Kai obviously picked up on that intention too, because he motioned for his boss to stand down. "I can take care of Lily. Between my mind control and her blood magic, anyone who messes with us will regret it. We've got the truce with the Skeleton Corps now, so there shouldn't be much of anyone coming at us on the streets regardless. You three should keep planning. The sooner we pull this 'party' off, the less time anyone has to get really suspicious."

Nox let out a disgruntled sound, but he settled for planting a quick but demanding kiss on my mouth. "You'll find her," he said firmly as he drew back.

As Kai and I went down to the motorcycles, my nerves started to jitter. The cool night air did nothing to chill me out. I squashed down my doubts as well as I could. My powers worked better when I was confident and focused, and this particular approach needed all my concentration.

Once I was sitting astride Kai's bike with one arm looped around his waist and the other ready to direct him, I closed my eyes and tapped into the hum of power inside me. My body shifted against his as I moved with the memories of the childhood play Marisol and I had so often gotten wrapped up in. The hum expanded through me, and I waited for the tug to come.

There was a faint quiver, somewhere in the distance

—so faint I couldn't tell for sure where it was coming from, like a sound you couldn't be sure you'd even heard at all.

I frowned and pushed the energies inside me harder, calling out to the harmony that linked my blood to Marisol's, all the common ties from our genetics. The sense of something in the distance wavered and pulsed, getting a little stronger just for a second and fading again. I still couldn't get a real lock on it.

"Start driving," I told Kai, swallowing my frustration. "Let's make a circuit of the outskirts of the city. I think they've taken her farther away—maybe I'll pick up her location better somewhere along the way."

Kai nodded without questioning me and took off down the street. For the first several minutes as we hurtled through the darkest side streets toward the edge of Mayfield, I let myself recover from my initial efforts, figuring there was no point in exhausting myself until I had a better chance.

When the shops and apartment buildings of the central city gave way to smaller apartment buildings mixed in with rows of crammed homes, and then those gave way to the more spread-out houses with lawns and driveways where city blended into suburb, Kai took a turn and started his circuit of the city. I dragged in a breath and summoned every shred of Marisol's essence in my mind again.

At first, I couldn't identify anything at all. I felt like a swimmer diving down meaning to tap the bottom of a pool, pulling and kicking and reaching and still only touching currents of water.

As Kai drove on, I finally caught the slightest tingling of an impression just beyond my mental fingertips. I groped at it, trying to cling on to it with everything I had. It expanded in my awareness, just a hint of a real tug now—

And then it dwindled away like a candle guttering out. What the hell?

I patted Kai's arm and called over the whir of the wind. "Turn around. Go back—go farther out from the city in the area we just passed through."

He veered around and shot down another street so fast my hair whipped out beneath the base of my helmet. I closed my eyes and stretched my senses again.

For the briefest instant, I thought I touched a tremor of *something*… and then it was gone again too.

My chest was starting to ache from how hard I was pushing myself, even though I hadn't done anything outwardly other than sit on the motorcycle seat. I gritted my teeth, but when I reached out again, I could feel all too clearly how my strength was flagging.

I motioned for Kai to stop. He parked by the corner of a quiet street, where a sprawling lawn stretched at least thirty feet before reaching a large house cast in thicker darkness by the shade of an oak tree. "Here?" he asked.

"No," I said, my throat constricting. "I still don't know. I couldn't get a good enough hold on her this time—not even as much as I got before."

He inclined his head thoughtfully. "They probably did take her out of the city, like you suspected. They could also be moving her around regularly to ensure she's difficult to track."

"But they can't be moving her around *constantly*," I protested, biting back a wail of frustration, and just then my phone rang in my pocket.

I yanked it out, and my heart stuttered. The caller ID said it was Marisol calling.

No one in the history of the universe has ever answered a phone faster. I flung the device to my ear, hitting the answer button at the same time. "Mare? Are you okay? Where are you?"

The voice that answered was definitely my sister's, but there was a hollow quality to her even tone that chilled me to the bone. "You need to leave me alone, Lily. I don't want to see you again. Stop trying to find me."

"What?" So many things I wanted to say jumbled together that it took me a second to fit my tongue around one. "You can't listen to them, Marisol. They're tricking you. I just want to—"

"Leave me *alone*!" Marisol snapped, and the phone line went dead.

I lowered my hand, my arm feeling abruptly feeble, like the muscles had turned to jelly. The Gauntts had put her up to placing that call, obviously. But they still had enough control over her to make her say those things, either because they were messing with her mind or because they'd threatened her into submission. My fingers squeezed around the phone so tightly I wouldn't have been surprised if I'd shattered the screen.

Kai was watching me. "They're keeping a very close eye on you," he said. "They must have known you'd left the apartment and at least suspected you were searching for her just now. The timing couldn't be a coincidence."

No, it probably couldn't. I glanced toward the star-flecked sky, my skin prickling with the sudden impression of being spied on from afar. "How would they do that?"

He shook his head. "There are lots of possibilities. We might be able to dodge them completely if we move you to a different location, get you a new phone, and keep you totally concealed… We'd have to get a new motorcycle or car to drive you around in, since they may have flagged the license plates. I'd have to talk to my tech guy about other options…"

All that, and it still might not work. The Gauntts had some idea what I was doing, and they'd already moved Marisol so far away that I'd barely picked up a trace of her location.

My head drooped. "If they're keeping tabs on me, there's no way we could be sure of them not following me. And you need to focus on dealing with the Skeleton Corps." My chest clenched tight, but I forced out the words. "We'll have to figure out another way. I don't think this strategy is going to get us anywhere. There's no point in trying just to fail all over again."

seventeen

Kai

L ily stayed quiet for the whole drive back into the center of the city. There was a limpness to the pressure of her arms around my chest that had my mind spinning on high alert, barely paying attention to my darkened surroundings other than the basics of traffic lights and stop signs.

Her failure to use her new powers to find her sister and her decision that it was hopeless to try again had obviously knocked her down. We Skullbreakers had made progress with our own problems, but we still hadn't managed to help our woman the way we'd meant to. The fucking Gauntts kept out-maneuvering us at every turn.

I cycled through the possibilities at the same speed

as the bike was whipping along the streets. The video had become a dead end. Lily's powers didn't extend far enough yet to make narrowing down her sister's location easy. Maybe we needed to work with her to exercise those powers and expand her abilities? But that could take quite a while.

Were there additional ways we could track down the Gauntts' other victims or learn more about what they did with them that could point us to Marisol's location? I might be able to weasel a little extra information out of the staff at Thrivewell who worked with the Gauntts most closely, although so far they hadn't provided much intel. I'd imagine a couple who'd been operating one of the biggest corporations in the country knew to keep their personal deviances separate from the workplace, or they wouldn't have made it this far without being exposed. You could only brainwash so many people at once.

Most of the information we'd gotten had come directly from their earlier victims. Fergus had revealed that Marie was involved too. That Skeleton Corps guy had led us to the spot along the marsh, which seemed important even if we didn't yet know why. The Gauntts' influence appeared to stretch far enough that a significant number of the Corps members had been affected. We'd found two already, after all. Who knew how many people in Mayfield carried their marks?

But we couldn't go around beating Corps guys into submission so we could check for marks and break them now that we were supposedly in a truce. That would set us right back to square one. I worked my jaw, adjusting my grip on the handlebars, and sucked in another breath laced with exhaust.

We *did* have a truce now. The Gauntts did appear to have affected several of their number. Maybe there were ways of using those facts that didn't require cracking open their memories one by one. After all, we didn't just need to know what the Gauntts were up to but also to have a way to beat *them* once we knew where to hit them.

I stewed on that line of thinking the rest of the way back to the apartment building. A giddy sense of anticipation, the high of a brilliant brainstorm, was tingling through me when I parked the bike. The second I helped Lily off, seeing the slump of her shoulders and her uncertain expression, my spirits deflated.

But this should brighten her up. I could offer her an alternate plan, one that would get us even farther toward destroying the couple who'd upended her and her sister's lives.

I grasped her hand and turned her all the way toward me. "It doesn't matter," I said. "We tried this one thing, and it didn't work out. Not every experiment is successful—that's how you narrow down your strategies. I have another one that should be even better."

She did perk up a little, her chin lifting and curiosity sparking in her eyes. "What's that?"

"For the moment, we've got the cooperation of the Skeleton Corps," I said. "We can turn them into allies in our war against the Gauntts. Go from having two different enemies to only one, and gaining a huge hammer to smash them with."

Lily's forehead furrowed. "Why would the Skeleton Corps want to take on a corporate giant? You convinced them not to attack *you* anymore, but it seems like it'd be pretty difficult to force them to attack someone else— on a larger scale, not just one guy Kai's persuaded. Especially when it's someone as powerful as the Gauntts."

Our enemies' ability to stay one—or five—steps ahead of us was wearing down her confidence too, clearly.

I rubbed my hands together, eager to show her just how simple this could be. "I'd be willing to bet that at least one high ranking member of the Skeleton Corps has one of those Gauntt marks and was messed with by them in who knows how many ways as a kid. We just figure out who—it might even be more than one of them—and break the seal. When all the memories come flooding back, they'll have plenty of their own motivation to take them on."

Lily still looked doubtful. "The one who's been through it will. I don't think they're going to want to admit to their buddies what happened to them. Gangsters don't like to look weak, do they?" She arched an eyebrow at me.

"Well, it'll give us one or two votes on our side, and then we've got our powers and yours to shove the others over the edge. After they see how we deal with people who've crossed us and our former murderers are out of their number, they'll have even more motivation."

I glanced down at a flicker of movement and found that a frog had hopped out of nowhere to leap onto the motorcycle's seat. For a second, I was tempted to take a page out of Lily's book and ask *it* to convince her that this plan was solid.

We'd defeat the Gauntts and save her sister. There was no if about it. I wouldn't even say "or die trying," because we'd already been there, done that, and come back stronger.

Lily stroked a finger over the frog's back and sagged against the side of the apartment building. The breeze stirred her hair, tossing stray strands across her lowered face. "I'm not saying it isn't worth trying. It just seems like it would still be so many steps away from rescuing Marisol. We don't even know what they might be doing to her already. How scared she must be. What pain she might be in."

When she looked so dejected, every bone in my body ached to tell her she didn't need to worry. That her sister was fine and would still be fine when we found her. That the Gauntts couldn't possibly win.

But the truth was, I didn't have the evidence to say that with the certainty I'd need to convince her. The failing was mine, no one else's. There was too much I *didn't* know, too much that was still out of my hands…

I looked down at those hands and then back at Lily, and my mind went abruptly still.

Was it really facts or evidence she needed? In the

past, I'd gotten caught up in my ideas of who she was and what was best for her, and those views had been too narrow. Just because I'd been around her for so much of her life, that didn't mean my instincts were automatically correct. I still had to really *see* her, recognize the cues she was giving off just as I would have with a stranger.

I couldn't let myself get so confident that I stopped taking her into account.

The frog croaked as if it'd picked up on my revelation and agreed with me. I studied Lily's posture and expression, taking in the details more thoroughly than I had before, the way I would have analyzed someone I needed to manipulate. In a sense, I wanted to manipulate Lily too, although not for ends of my own. Only to figure out what I could best offer that would bring her out of this despondent state.

What I saw hit me like a punch to the gut. She was withdrawing into herself, hugging herself, bracing herself against the wall—because she didn't feel she could lean on me that way?

Because facts and strategies weren't what she needed to hold her up right now, and that was all I was offering.

I wasn't Ruin, not by a long shot. PDAs had never come naturally to me. Getting turned on and acting on my desire was one thing. Figuring out how to show Lily I was here for her in every way she needed?

Why did that feel so hard when it should be so simple?

I had a perfect model for that kind of affection and

support, though. What *would* Ruin have done if he'd seen Lily like this? What would he have said?

I wanted to be that for her too. I wanted her to know she could count on all of us when her hopes started to falter.

Stepping closer, I slipped my arms around her and drew her closer to me. My hand came up to stroke over her soft hair, and she tucked her head against my shoulder instinctively. She stayed a bit tensed, as if she was afraid I'd let her go if she pressed into the embrace too much, but gradually, as I hugged her tighter, her body relaxed against mine.

My throat had roughened for reasons I couldn't explain. I tried to clear it, but my voice still came out a bit ragged. "No matter what happens, I'll stand by you. We all will. We're in this however you need us, all the way to the end."

Lily made a slightly choked sound and dared to hug me harder. Some part of me wanted to stiffen up in turn, but I willed my stance to stay loose, my hold firm but tender. Maybe this sort of attitude didn't come naturally to me, but I meant it. I cared about her so much I wanted to storm over to the Gauntts' house right now and slice'n'dice the bunch of them just to relieve that worry hanging over her head. I *would* have, if I'd thought I could see a plan like that through.

When she mattered that much to me, offering a goddamn *hug* wasn't any kind of trial.

"I don't know how I'd have gotten through this if it

wasn't for all of you," she mumbled against my shoulder.

I couldn't help chuckling. "I'd imagine *some* parts of your life would have been significantly simpler."

"Maybe. But there'd have been so much I didn't realize, so much still wrong that I didn't even know how to start tackling. I'm glad you guys came back into my life. I'm glad I have *you*, even if I argue sometimes."

I pressed a kiss to her temple. "Arguing is good. It keeps my mind sharp and makes sure I have all of my facts and explanations in order."

I felt her smile against my skin. "Well, I'm glad you see it that way. I guess we should go upstairs so you can go over the new plan with the other guys and get started on making it happen?"

"Is that what you want?" I asked, even though my first impulse was to do just what she'd said. "There's nothing wrong with needing a moment or two for yourself."

"I think I've gotten that." She eased away from me and then touched my cheek, bobbing up on her feet to press her mouth to mine. It was the sweetest kiss I'd ever exchanged with her, nothing like the urgent passion that'd flowed between us before—but right then, I wasn't sure I didn't like this one even better.

My decision to pause and really take in the situation carried with me as we headed up to the apartment. When we stepped inside, I found myself taking stock of my three colleagues in a way I might not have in quite some time.

Nox and Ruin were easy to read. They weren't really ones to keep their emotions close to their chests. Ruin bounded over to ask Lily how our search had gone and immediately enveloped her in a hug that was probably ten times more comforting than mine. I would just stick to believing that it was the thought that counted. Nox stalked around making growly remarks about all the things he intended to do to the Gauntts when he got his hands on them. Straightforward enough.

But Jett hung back from our group by a few steps, his eyes dark and a slight uncertainty to his posture. I wasn't seeing the same conflicted restraint in him as before Nox had somehow shaken him out of his resistance to getting physical with Lily, but he didn't look entirely at ease all the same. What was up with him?

Before, I might have dismissed it as his own problem to worry about. I'd been putting my brains toward tackling our enemies, not my friends. But it stood to reason that we'd make more headway with the former if the latter had less weighing on them.

From the little bit of distance he was keeping from us, I'd almost say he didn't think he belonged with us, not totally. Which seemed ridiculous, but my observations were rarely inaccurate.

I let Ruin and Nox continue heaping affection and promises of vengeance on Lily and went over to join the artist. Jett noticed me coming and ran a hand through his purple hair, straightening at the same time as if he'd pulled himself up by his scalp. He was trying to hide his discomfort from me, which was even more of a sign that he wasn't at ease with us.

Did he feel left out because his powers weren't as easily applicable in a fight as ours? Like he'd become the weakest link? That seemed like the most probable explanation.

I clapped a hand to his shoulder—tentatively, because one hug had hardly turned me into a master of physical demonstration. "You know, I should have said it earlier—that was some pretty amazing work you did against the Skeleton Corps dudes who stormed in here the other night—I saw the nose reshaping on that one guy while we were moving the bodies. Talk about rhinoplasty." I chuckled.

Jett looked at me as if he was wondering whether some totally new ghost had kicked the Kai he knew out of this body and taken it over for itself. "Thanks?" he said, like a question.

I groped for the right words to say. It was never hard to figure them out with people I didn't give a shit about. With the few who did, my tongue didn't seem to work quite right.

I gave him a little shake that should have conveyed manly affection. "We make an impressive team, all four of us. I'm going to incorporate your abilities more into our plans going forward. And I've always appreciated what you bring to the Skullbreakers. Just so you know."

Jett's puzzled expression didn't totally fade, but a hint of a smile crossed his lips. "All right," he said. "I guess that's a good thing to know." He cracked his knuckles. "And I'm ready to rearrange all the faces that need it, as literally as possible."

I laughed. "Sounds good to me." Now we just needed to rearrange our former enemies into our greatest weapon against the Gauntts.

eighteen

Lily

"I still don't think they're going to jump for joy at the idea that we want to examine their armpits," I had to say as I tramped with the Skullbreakers over to the venue where we were meeting the Skeleton Corps leadership this time. This spot seemed a little more traditional than the ice cream parlor. The sign out front read *Crow's Feet Tattoos*, which didn't sound like the most stunning endorsement for the shop's services, but who knew what people were into these days?

"If they complain about it, I can work my way through them one by one," Kai pointed out without a hint of concern. I didn't know what'd gotten into him yesterday when he'd turned huggy all of a sudden—not that I'd minded—but he'd had a looser energy to him since then, like maybe he'd needed the hug as much as I had.

"They might complain even more about you going around hitting all of them when we're supposed to have a truce," I muttered.

"As soon as we find one of the big bosses who the Gauntts messed with and get him to remember what they did, it'll be a piece of cake," Nox said with his typically impervious air. He strode right up to the front of the tattoo shop and pushed the door wide, though I could see his muscles flex in preparation for an attack.

In theory, this meet-up was to discuss final preparations for the "party" the Skullbreakers were supposedly throwing to celebrate their murderers in a couple of days. I wasn't totally sure what all Nox and the others had told the Skeleton Corps leaders to convince them of their good intentions, but it appeared to have worked. We walked into the shop to find four of the men we'd confronted in the ice cream parlor as well as several underlings gathered in the far end of the room, beyond the tattoo chair.

They held no weapons, but seeing all those underlings sent an uneasy prickle over my skin. Were they here just for defense in case my guys got out of line, or were the Corps bosses less sure about this truce than they'd claimed to be?

The five of us stopped at the front of the store near the door and windows, both of which I supposed could make for a quick getaway if need be, although one significantly more painful than the other. Ruin gave the Skeleton Corps contingent a grin and a little wave, which was only met with glowers that didn't appear to faze him at all. Jett started shooting glances at the spread of designs tacked to the side wall, the twist of his mouth suggesting he'd have liked to revamp at least a few of them.

"Well, we're here," one of the Corps leaders said in an irritated voice. "What was so important?"

Nox drew himself up with a hint of swagger. "We'll get to the most important business in a second. I promise you that you'll be glad you stuck around for that. First, have you rounded up all your members for the bash this weekend? We want to make sure no one who helped end the Skullbreakers misses out on the celebration."

"It's pretty weird that you're so obsessed with a two-bit gang that bit the dust twenty years ago," another of the men snarked. I saw Kai bite his tongue against correcting him to twenty-*one* years.

Nox snorted as if the comment was ridiculous. "You don't know our history. Getting rid of those assholes had a *huge* impact on our lives. We'd be totally different people if it wasn't for your... help." He offered a broad smirk, clearly pleased with himself for the double meaning behind his words that they couldn't piece together.

The third man eyed us up and down. "What, did they steal your pacifier out of the cradle? You're still practically kids."

Ruin chuckled. "We're young at heart, but older than we look! The best way to be."

"It wasn't just us but people who came before us," Kai put in. "Like we've said, there's a lot of history we've only just finished dealing with."

"Anyway," Ruin added, "who doesn't like a party? You all get to come."

I felt like I should say something too, as the most normal member of the group, if only to show that we were all on board with this. I cleared my throat. "We're handling everything. All you need to do is show up and have a good time. It's kind of a celebration of the truce too, right?"

The Skeleton Corps guys shifted on their feet, looking like they weren't totally sure the truce was something worth celebrating and not cursing. But they didn't bother arguing anymore.

"We've gotten names and tapped people so they'll turn up," the first man said grudgingly. "There aren't a whole lot still with us, one way or another, but they'll be there."

"Perfect." Nox rubbed his hands together. "It'll be a spectacular time."

"What's this other important business you needed to bring up?" the second man demanded.

"Right." Nox fixed his gaze on each of them in turn. "We've found out that a whole bunch of your people, including at least one of you, has a common enemy that we share. Someone who messed with you without you even knowing it. We figured in the spirit of our truce, we should pass on that info and give you the chance to do something about it."

He was making a bit of a gamble. We couldn't be absolutely sure that one of the Skeleton Corps leaders had come under the Gauntts' sway as a kid. But it seemed like one out of every few guys we'd encountered in their lower levels had been marked, and the bosses were young enough—late thirties and forties, from the looks of them—that the Gauntts would have been adults when they were the right age. We didn't know when Nolan and Marie had gotten started on their bizarre game, but it'd obviously been going on for a while.

And if none of them had a mark, then there were plenty of underlings we could work with too.

The fourth man—the oldest of the Corps bosses, who'd been silent until now—folded his arms over his chest and scoffed. "You don't think we'd *notice* if someone had been messing with us? How the fuck could you know more about what's happening to us than we do?"

Nox shrugged. "How the fuck can we make you follow our orders or punch you from across a room? You're smart enough to be able to see that there are powers you didn't know existed until now, aren't you? We're not the only ones in town who have them—and the other people who do are a lot shittier than us."

"And they can get into your head so you can't remember," I said.

All four of the Corps leaders looked at us with

194

uncertain skepticism. They couldn't deny what Nox had said about supernatural powers, but it didn't surprise me that they'd also be reluctant to accept that they needed us to give them an FYI about their own enemies.

"Well, spit it out," the first guy said eventually.

Nox tipped his head toward them. "Any of you remember getting visits from members of the Gauntt family back when you were a kid?"

Opening with that question got us exactly what we needed without any of them even answering it, at least with words. Most of the men standing across from us responded with expressions of varying degrees of confusion. But two of them—the third of the bosses and one of the underlings on the fringes of the group—tensed up. The boss recovered quickly, smoothing out his reaction as if nothing had happened, but if I'd caught the blip, he had no hope of Kai's sharp eyes missing it.

Kai pointed at him. "You did. They got to you—Nolan or Marie or both of them."

The other guys looked at him, a murmur of consternation moving through the bunch. The man's thin eyebrows drew together as he postured with apparent anger. "I don't know what the fuck you're talking about. No one's gotten one up on me. There's nothing wrong with my head."

"You have a mark," I said quietly, and the others fell silent so that my voice carried through the room. "Somewhere on your upper arm, probably the underside, about the size of a nickel, like a birthmark."

Again, there was a brief twitch of discomfort before he schooled his face into his preferred mask of indignance. "Get the fuck out of here. Now you're just making up bullshit."

Ruin's good cheer dropped away in an instant. "Lily doesn't *lie*," he said fiercely.

I waved for him to stand down and focused on the Corps guy. "I had one too," I said. "I managed to break through it so that I could remember what they blocked in my mind. I've done it for a couple of other Skeleton Corps men since then—lower-level guys. I can do it for you too. You *want* to know what they really did to you, don't you? How they might be controlling you even now? How can you run the Corps if someone else is running *you*?"

I'd used those words partly to convince his colleagues rather than him, so they'd turn on the pressure for him to comply. Weirdly, they all started to draw themselves up in a blustering show of authority, as if I'd somehow offended them.

"If he says there's nothing, then there's nothing," the fourth man said. "We didn't come here to listen to crazy stories."

"You don't know shit about any of us," the second agreed.

Nox let out a disdainful huff. "If you're not going to let us open your eyes willingly, then we'll just have to wrench them open. We can't have a truce with someone under the influence of the enemy."

Several of the Skeleton Corps guys moved their

hands to guns partly concealed at their sides. "And how exactly do you think you're going to make us?" the third leader sneered.

Nox smirked at him. "Like this."

He whipped his hand out through the air and yanked it back in a fist so abruptly that a couple of the underlings flinched. It hadn't come within more than a few feet of the other men—but his talents were clearly expanding, and they hadn't been prepared that he could *pull* with his supernatural abilities as well as *punch*.

Electricity quivered through the air, and the third boss's shirt shot out from his body as if it'd been grabbed—because it had, by fingers of ghostly energy. He staggered forward across the space between us. The next second, Kai was smacking him in the head. "Stand still with Lily and keep your mouth shut."

That took care of our main target. But as he jerked to a halt next to me by the dingy shop window, the other Skeleton Corps members took aim as if we were kidnapping him rather than trying to break a magic spell on him. Which, to be fair, was probably a much more common occurrence in the criminal underworld.

Nox shoved me to the side so that the Corps guy would shield me from his colleagues' bullets if they started firing, and then all four of the Skullbreakers sprang into action.

Nox whipped out his fists, sending pistols jerking aside and in some cases clattering to the ground before their owners could get a shot off. Jett dashed in there fast enough to slap his hands against weapons still clutched in people's hands, altering the shapes of guns and knives alike. Suddenly the Skeleton Corps crew found themselves holding metal giraffes, wiener dogs, and butterflies as if a demented balloon-animal artist had swept through.

Ruin delivered a couple of blows that had two of the underlings lunging at their colleagues, snarling like feral wolves. Kai couldn't try to control anyone else while his power needed to work on my target, so he settled for landing a punch here and a kick there the old-fashioned way.

But it wasn't quite enough. Even with all the chaos careening through the room, the fourth of the Corps bosses kept his grip on his gun. He aimed it straight at Nox's head while Nox was grappling with a couple of underlings who'd tossed their gun-animals aside.

A cry ripped up my throat. "No!" And energy surged out of me alongside the protest, snatching around the blood flowing through the man's chest and squeezing it into his heart.

I hadn't meant to work the bloody part of my powers on anyone today. Seeing the guy seize up and sway, his skin graying, made me feel sick even though I'd watched this play out a few times already. Even though I knew I was saving Nox's life.

This wasn't how I wanted to save *anyone's* life—by holding someone else's in my hands, almost literally. But I didn't have much choice, did I?

"Stop," I said, my voice carrying over the clamor. "Stop fighting and tell the rest of your men to stop. I don't want to detonate your heart, but I will if I have to."

The Skeleton Corps guy turned his gaze on me, his eyes wide. He coughed and shook. "Enough," he said raggedly. "Fall back."

His submission gave me a queasy sense of satisfaction. The other two bosses stared at him for a second, but they must have been pretty rattled already. They hollered to the underlings, and as their people drew back, the Skullbreakers retreated to our side of the room too.

The Corps didn't know that I couldn't work my bloody magic when I was concentrating on breaking a mark, and hopefully they wouldn't get to find out that fact today. Without wasting any time, I jerked up the sleeve of the third boss, who was still standing rigidly by me. I raised his arm so the others could see the pink splotch right where I'd said it'd be on his upper arm.

"I'm going to break the supernatural power in this, and then he'll remember," I said. "That's *all* I'm going to do as long as the rest of you behave yourselves."

"And you should definitely listen to her," Ruin put in.

The Corps members stirred uneasily but stayed where they were. I closed my hands around the man's bicep and threw all the energy humming inside me at the mark.

Each time I did it, this procedure got easier in every way. I was starting to know how to hit the Gauntts' magical barrier at the angles that would crack it the fastest, to sense the weakening spots the second they started to give and focus more energy there. Closing my eyes, I rammed all the power I had at the wall they'd set up around those memories in the guy's mind.

I'd barely broken a sweat when the barrier shattered apart. The guy sucked a sharp breath through his nose, since Kai had told him to shut his mouth. He let out an anguished-sounding grunt.

Kai gave him a light swat. "You can talk but don't attack any of us."

The man's lips burst apart. "Those *fuckers*," he said, his voice raw with both anger and horror. He bobbed back and forth on his feet for a few seconds before focusing his eyes on his colleagues across from us. "These guys are telling the truth. The Gauntts— We've got to destroy those pricks. Burn them to the fucking ground."

nineteen

Ruin

Lily put her hand over the mouthpiece part of the phone and let out a faint groan before she went back to the conversation. "Yes, I understand that the apartment was a little messy. That's why I'm giving up the damage deposit. But all the stuff you're talking about already wasn't working when I moved in. I can show you multiple emails where I pointed those problems out to you. I'm not paying any more money."

I stopped where I'd been wandering around the apartment, munching on my spicy beef jerky, and took in her tense expression. She'd been on the phone with her former landlord for several minutes now, fending off his attempts to suggest that the poor water pressure and leaky kitchen sink and who knew what else were somehow her fault.

"Do you want me to go deal with him?" I whispered with a lift of my eyebrows, drawing my finger across my throat to make my meaning clear. It would be my pleasure to end his harassment of our woman in the most final way possible.

To my disappointment, Lily shook her head. She rolled her eyes at whatever the landlord said next and slumped farther into the sofa cushions. "Yes, I understand, but that wasn't my responsibility."

I swallowed the last of the jerky, not enjoying its intense flavor as much as usual. I didn't like to see Lily stressed out at all, and in the past few days her spirits had seemed... darker than usual. Like there was a shadow over her. Something in her eyes when she stopped our enemies in their tracks by manipulating their blood, something in her expression and stance afterward that suggested she was hardening herself.

I liked her soft, sweet, and smiling. If she'd been happier taking on a harsh role, I'd have supported that all the way too. But the smiles had been coming few and far between.

Looking at her pose on the sofa, an idea sparked in my mind of one very simple strategy for bringing more light into her life. A fiery sort of light.

Unable to restrain a grin, I walked over to her and knelt by her feet. Lily jerked her gaze to me, knitting her brow. *What are you doing?* she mouthed silently.

"What does it look like?" I murmured back, and

stroked my fingers over her knees. She was still wearing just her long sleep shirt that she'd spent the night in, which worked just fine for my purposes. "You need someone to counterbalance the awfulness you're having to listen to."

"Not like—" She cut herself off when she needed to respond to the landlord. "Of course. But my security deposit covers that. I looked at the lease."

While she spoke, I teased my fingers higher up her thighs and kissed the inside of her knee. Lily shifted her legs as if to close her thighs, but I nudged between them before she could and caught her eyes with a challenge in mine. "If you don't like me doing this while you're on the phone, tell him you're done and get off. *I'm* not done."

"Ruin," she muttered, but a huskier note crept into her voice alongside the irritation. When I flicked my tongue against her inner thigh, her breath caught with a restrained gasp. Whether consciously or not, she scooted just a little farther down on the sofa toward me.

I tugged her sleep shirt up to her waist and traced my fingers over the curves of her ass through her thin panties. The smell of her filled my nose, the perfect muskiness of her desire mixing with her usual wildflower scent. There wasn't any better snack than this.

I kissed a trail up her thigh, closer and closer to her pussy. Lily squirmed. When she spoke into the phone next, her voice quavered just slightly. "Right, but it was already like that. I keep telling you—"

Without warning her, I tugged the crotch of her panties aside and planted my mouth right on her cunt. Lily's voice cut off with the start of a whimper that she covered with a swift clap of her hand over her mouth. As I lapped at her from slit to clit, her legs started to tremble. Her chest hitched as she struggled to steady her breath.

"I'm fine," she managed to say. "I'm just"—a muffled gasp—"tired of listening to this bullshit. I've paid more than enough. Don't call me again."

Just as she hung up, I sucked on her clit with renewed force. Lily bucked against me with a moan she could now let out and slammed the phone down on the cushions next to her. Her fingers dug into my hair.

"You are the worst," she grumbled, and panted while I drank up the juices trickling out of her with another swipe of my tongue. "Don't stop."

I had no intention of even slowing down. I devoured her, grazing my teeth over her clit, curling my tongue right inside her opening, working my lips against her until she was outright writhing. The scratch of her fingernails against my scalp set off jolts of electricity that shot straight to my groin.

My cock throbbed for attention, but this moment was just for her. Just for my Lily. She needed to remember how precious she was.

A whine of need slipped from Lily's throat, I clamped down on her with even more vigor, and her thighs tightened around my head as she arched into her release.

She lay there, sagging against the sofa, for several seconds. Then, as I raised my head, she gave me a light swat. "Don't go around distracting me like that."

My mouth stretched into another grin. "I'll make sure to do it as often as possible."

"You…" she growled, and sat up straighter again, her sleep shirt falling back into place. Her eyes flashed, but there was as much passion as frustration there—an eager energy I hadn't seen in her in days.

I pushed myself back from the sofa and onto my feet. There were more games we could play. "What are you going to do about it? Teach me a lesson?"

More heat flared in Lily's gaze. She shoved herself upright with a predatory grace. "And would that work?"

"Oh, I think definitely so," I replied. "But you'll have to catch me first."

She took a grab at me, and I was off like a shot, dashing for her bedroom. Lily darted after me, her bare feet thumping across the floorboards. Abruptly, I was insanely grateful to be alone in the apartment with her just this once while the other guys finalized our party preparations. I didn't mind sharing our woman—I *loved* seeing her quake with the combined pleasure we could bring her to—but there was something to be said for the moments when I had her all to myself.

I spun around as I reached the foot of the bed, and Lily crashed into me. She pushed me backward without any real resistance and glowered down at me as she pinned me to the mattress, straddling my hips and bracing her hands against my shoulders.

I beamed up at her, knowing I could have displaced her in an instant if I'd wanted to, not having the slightest desire to do so. "Okay, you caught me. What will my punishment be?"

A mischievous smile crossed Lily's lips. She rocked her pussy against me, taking me from semi-rigid to stiff as steel with the torturous friction. "What if I don't want to punish you? What if I just want to make sure you finish what you started?"

My own breath was getting a bit rough now. "I think I could be on board with that," I teased.

"Hmph," she said, and trailed her fingers down my torso to the waist of my jeans. The heel of her hand skimmed over the button and swiveled against my already straining erection. "You think? I want you completely, one hundred percent, rock-solid on this."

A ragged laugh spilled out of me. "I'm definitely there."

"Good." She unzipped my fly and tugged down my pants and boxers to free me. As her hand rubbed up and down my cock, I tipped my head back with a groan. No other woman had ever touched me anywhere near as well as she did.

I wanted to be in her slickness right now, rocking her to another release, without any barriers between us. But I had Nox's voice in the back of my head reminding me to be careful.

Kai could probably have gotten away with it, at least if Lily had gotten on some kind of birth control. His host hadn't seemed to have much of a social life. But the popular guy I'd possessed had clearly gotten around. I couldn't trust whatever was left of him to be clean even if *I* hadn't been with another woman in two decades.

Lily wasn't one to throw caution totally to the wind anyway, no matter how much fun we were having. Without my having to say anything, she crawled over me up the bed, letting her breasts graze my chest through her sleep shirt, and grabbed a condom out of the bedside table. "Rock-hard and all wrapped up."

"And ready to be in you," I said, clutching her hips as she resumed her previous position.

She hummed to herself and stroked her fingers up and down my cock several more times, pausing only to tease them over my balls as well, until I felt like I was going to explode. Then, finally, she eased the condom over me and sank down to welcome me in.

Having the firm warmth of her channel close around me always felt like coming home. My breath stuttered as I bucked up to meet her halfway, and Lily let out a gasp she didn't have to hide this time.

She leaned forward, splaying her hands against my chest this time, and rode me at her own pace. The first slow, steady sways of her body had me groaning and my balls clenching already. But I held on, intending to be there with her until the end, no matter how deliciously torturous she made the journey there.

As she sped up, the ache expanded through my groin. Her breath started to fracture. I gazed up at her, my heart swelling with affection even as my cock did with lust. "That's right, Angelfish. Take everything you need. I'm right here with you."

She whimpered and bucked even faster. Her eyelids drooped as she chased her release. I brought my thumb to her clit, circling it against that nub as she bobbed up and down, and her fingers curled against my chest. With a cry and a shudder, her pussy clamped around me.

The second I felt her come, my dick flooded her. A torrent of heat surged through me and left me sprawling boneless on the bed. But I had enough strength left to tug her down into my embrace.

"Good enough revenge?" I asked.

Lily snorted. "You never get phone calls. I can't pay you back properly." She paused, tucking herself more closely against me with her head bent next to mine. Her fingers drifted along my arm. "You haven't talked to Ansel's family since the last time we went over there, have you?"

The memory of the confrontation with my host's mother made my stomach clench up. I wrapped my arm around Lily and breathed in her scent until my insides relaxed again. "No. Kai figured out how to block numbers on our phones and showed me. I don't want to talk to them ever again."

"You got really upset about them letting the Gauntts get at Ansel when he was a kid," Lily said hesitantly. "I've never seen you like that otherwise."

I could hear the implied question in that statement, but it took me a minute to figure out the best way to answer it. I rolled toward her and pulled her right against me, burying my face in her hair.

"I don't like getting upset that way," I said. "It doesn't do anyone any good, really. It's not like getting angry when someone hurts you, because then I'm defending you. Nothing I do changes anything that happened years ago."

"But you did get upset. And that's okay. You don't have to always be upbeat about everything. I was just surprised because it's not as if you *liked* Ansel."

"He was a jerk," I said automatically, and mulled a little more. The full story might make Lily sad—but on the other hand, it'd help her understand, which could make her feel better. And she was asking.

I wanted to make her happy, but I also wanted to be honest with her.

"I guess it reminded me too much of things about my own family," I said. "They weren't... They weren't *awful* like I think Nox's and Jett's were. They didn't hurt me. They just... didn't do anything for me at all. They'd tell me to go off and get into whatever made me happy, and then they'd get into whatever *they* wanted for themselves, even if they hadn't bothered to give me breakfast or make sure I had shoes that fit or whatever."

I heard Lily's frown in her voice. "I think that is hurting you. Kids need someone to take care of them. It's not exactly optional. Even my mom and Wade at least made sure that Marisol and I got regular meals and proper clothes."

I shrugged. "I got by. Sometimes I was hungry and

sometimes I was cold—and a lot of the time I was lonely—but it could have been a lot worse. And the more I looked at the positive side, thinking about all the things I could do whenever I wanted since they weren't really paying attention, the less the bad stuff bothered me."

Lily pressed a kiss to my cheek. "So you got in the habit of always being positive about everything," she said softly.

"It's a lot easier to be happy that way," I told her. "Why should I let what someone else did get me down? I didn't need them in the end. I got through it, and here I am."

"But it must still bother you a little, or what Ansel's parents did wouldn't have upset you."

"Yeah." I cocked my head against the pillow. "Something about the thought of them just looking the other way, not caring what those assholes did to him right there in their own home... Even my parents didn't step *that* far back. They had things they'd rather do than take care of me, but they didn't offer me up for someone else's abuse. And it was hard enough, at least at first, to feel good about things even the way I had it. Ansel was a jerk when I took him over, but he must have been pretty miserable as a kid too. When he could still remember what happened to him."

"It would have been pretty hard to see a positive side to anything the Gauntts were doing," Lily agreed. "His mom deserved everything you said and everything you made her feel about herself. I was just worried about you. If being cheerful about everything is what feels best to you, then cheer away. Nobody can take that away from you."

I smiled and nuzzled her face. "They can't take it away from you either, Waterlily. Don't let anyone or anything bring you down."

"How can I, when I've got you?" Lily said with a chuckle, but I couldn't help suspecting I hadn't so much cured her of the darkness that'd gripped her as only gotten it to lift for a little while.

twenty

Lily

The medieval-themed restaurant that the Skullbreakers had taken over as their new clubhouse had once been atmospherically dim. Now, there were lights everywhere I looked. Electric lanterns along the tables at the edges of the room. Flashing neon fixtures up by the ceiling. Even the throne where I'd had a very good time with Nox and Ruin what felt like a century ago was now smothered in strands of fairy lights.

Thankfully, there was also plenty of food, because the Skullbreaker guys could plow through an entire royal feast just on their own. So they'd had their associates bring in enough platters to count as approximately three feasts, one of which they'd already made short work of. I really hoped none of the Skeleton Corps members had particularly been looking forward to jalapeno poppers or spicy nachos.

The Corps members were trickling in, taking in the décor, the food, and the blaring disco music someone had thought it was a good idea to put on with expressions that ranged from skeptical to horrified. It might have been partly to do with the uninhibited dance Ruin was currently doing in the center of the cleared floor beyond the throne. He was gyrating away like he'd now been possessed by the spirit of John Travolta, grinning the whole time.

I smoothed down the skirt of my dress, like I'd already done about a million times. I'd felt the need to dress up at least a little to match the supposed occasion, even though I didn't feel entirely comfortable in fancier clothes—although this was definitely a casual frock, not some ballgown—and it'd required I'd drive my car here rather than riding with one of the guys. Fred 2.0 had been getting neglected anyway.

Ruin boogeyed into another song. I elbowed Nox where he was standing next to me. "Shouldn't we, I don't know, put on some tunes from at least this *century*? Were *you* even born when this one came out?"

Nox scoffed. "My gram would have taken mortal offense to you criticizing the great Bee Gees. We couldn't figure how to download stuff onto our phones, and this was the only CD we could come up with that was reasonably party-like. It won't matter in a few minutes anyway."

Because in less than half an hour, he planned on the main musical accompaniment to the evening being gunshots.

He moved away from me to motion some of the Skullbreakers recruits onto the floor so Ruin didn't look quite so lonely. Jett immediately came up at my other side, a cola in one hand and a churro in the other. I raised an eyebrow at him. "Am I being babysat?"

He gave me a small smile that sent a tingle of warmth through my chest—just the fact that he would stand that close to me and smile with such open affection, even if it was still tempered by his usual taciturn reserve.

"You're the deadliest person in this room," he said. "You should be babysitting us."

That might be true, but it turned the tingle into a twitch of my nerves. I folded my arms over my chest, not wanting to stress about whether the guys could pull off their plan without a hitch while the targets of that plan were now spreading out through the restaurant. When hugging myself didn't dampen my restlessness, I gnawed on a slice of pizza instead, careful to avoid the pie Ruin had ordered smothered with hot peppers.

"I assume you're all sure who the guests of honor are?" I said in a low voice. They didn't want to slaughter *all* of the Skeleton Corps guys, only the few who'd been involved in their own murders.

Kai had just joined us at my other side, catching my question. He answered instead of Jett—he probably had an itemized list in his back pocket. "It seems there are five Corps members still in this world who were involved in the incident we're 'celebrating.' They're all supposed to be here tonight. We've arranged special seats for them with name tags and everything." He tipped his head toward the banquet table in front of the throne. "I've seen four out of those five so far."

"It looks like the leadership decided to come," I remarked. Three men I recognized from the ice cream parlor had already arrived, and one more was just strolling in. Of the missing two—not including the guy who'd died in the fighting, of course—one was probably in the hospital after the lessons in hospitality the Skullbreakers had given him, and the other...

The other was the one with the mark whose memories I'd unlocked a couple of days ago.

I frowned, scanning the crowd in case I'd simply failed to notice him. There were at least fifty people spread out through the restaurant now, eating and gabbing even if they weren't quite into the dancing yet —half of them Skullbreaker associates and half from the Skeleton Corps. After getting so up close and personal with the marked guy, I was sure I'd have recognized him.

A shiver ran through my stomach, but it was probably just nerves. There wasn't anything all that odd about him passing up the party. I was surprised by how many of the top brass *had* shown up. He might come later. Or he might be in a therapy session getting help for those years of suppressed trauma.

Probably better that he wasn't here to have tonight's events add to that load.

I gulped the last of the pizza slice and felt some regret about the lump it'd formed in my stomach. I didn't think my digestive system was going to be functioning properly again until this night was over.

Kai straightened up a bit, his gaze flicking to the front of the room. "There's the last of them. The pricks who mowed us down." More emotion than I usually heard from him wound through his voice. He might be treating this event as a mind game of sorts, but he was just as pissed off as the others about his untimely death twenty—excuse me, twenty-*one*—years ago.

I watched the latest arrival: a pudgy, balding man who looked like these days he must have conducted most of his gangster activities by yelling at people lower down the ladder to do his bidding. He walked tentatively along the table against the opposite wall, picking up a plate and helping himself to several mini spring rolls. His expression as he took in the space looked as skeptical as that on many of the others.

Kai clearly picked up on the same vibe. "I'm going to nudge Nox," he said, pushing away from the table. "We need to get this show on the road before any of them decide the party's not their jive and take off on us."

I glanced over at Jett, who took another gulp of his cola. "Do you need to help rounding everyone up?"

He shrugged and swiped his hair away from his eyes. "Nah. Nox and Kai can get everyone in place. My main contribution is going to be in the big reveal." A small, feral grin curled his lips. It was disturbingly sexy. Or at least, I had the sense that I should have been disturbed by how sexy I found it, even if I wasn't actually.

Ruin was still tearing up the dance floor, although at least he had some company now, awkwardly bobbing and swaying along without quite as much enthusiasm. Nox ushered the guests of honor past the dancers to their special table. They brought plates of food with them, and Kai hustled over with a few of the larger platters and then liquor bottles so they could help themselves without getting up. By all appearances, they were eager to pamper the five Skullbreakers murderers.

When the guests of honor were settled in and eating away, if still with somewhat puzzled faces, Nox made a brusque gesture. The music cut out. He clapped his hands, and Jett left my side to stand next to the others as they formed a line across from the banquet table.

Nox grinned broadly. "Gentlemen," he said, with the slightest of sarcastic sneers. "We're so glad that those of you who played a role in destroying the Skullbreakers two decades ago could join us today. We have an even more special surprise for you! If you'd just—"

He never got to say what he wanted them to do, because at that moment, the paneled ceiling broke open, and at least two dozen men in skeleton-print ski masks dropped down into the party with guns already firing. In an instant, it was literally raining men—and bullets.

The crowd broke apart with yells and brandishes of their own guns. As the shots thundered in my ears, I dove under one of the tables.

Peering out from beneath it, I couldn't help noticing that the Skeleton Corps men who'd already been part of the festivities didn't look particularly surprised. *They'd* all gathered at the front of the restaurant, other than the five at the head table, and they were yanking their own guns out now.

Ruin ducked under the table next to me, grabbing my arm. "Are you okay?"

"Yeah," I said. "But what the hell are we going to do?" It was utter chaos out there, bodies jerking and falling on both sides, people scrambling to find whatever cover they could. Several of the lights shattered in the hail of bullets, darkening the room and making it harder to follow the action.

"We've been double-double-crossed!" Ruin exclaimed. "Triple-crossed? Before we could even get to the double-crossing part!" His head jerked toward the table by the throne, and he must have noticed a couple of the men there bracing as if to make a dash for the doors. He bared his teeth fiercely. "We can't let *them* get away."

I was going to say that we really should focus on getting out of here alive ourselves and worry about the whole murderous revenge thing later, but Ruin had already scrambled out from under the table and dashed over to stop the guests of honor from making their escape.

The front doors burst open behind the main group of Corps members, and several of the Skullbreakers recruits pumped bullets into the mass of bodies. They'd been stationed outside to make sure the targets of our revenge didn't get away, but they'd obviously realized they were needed inside now.

A bunch of the Skeleton Corps members crumpled, but others flung themselves out of the way in time and shot back. Our own guys tumbled over with sprays of blood. I couldn't tell who was even winning.

Why had the Corps turned on us? Had they figured out what the Skullbreakers were up to? Maybe one of those recruits had decided it was worth the risk of tattling on us so they could get in good with the original higher power in the city.

There was no way to know right now. The hum of supernatural energy inside me prickled all the way to my skin, and I threw it toward all the liquid I could easily reach. I pelted liquor bottles and pop cans into every masked figure I could see still standing and anyone else I was sure was Skeleton Corps. It seemed like a faster way to deal with the horde of attackers than trying to explode their hearts one by one.

So then there were bottles and cans as well as bullets flying every which way and sometimes colliding, and more people ended up sheltering under the tables and behind the throne and pinball machine than out on the floor. A stray bullet shattered the glass top of the pinball machine, and I heard a groan of horror that was probably from Nox.

The gangsters were still shooting from beneath and around their hiding places. A guy lunged at me out of nowhere and immediately regretted it when I instinctively wrenched at his blood with all the power I had in me. His body seized up in mid-spring, streaks of crimson spurted out of his nose, and he sprawled on the floor next to me with his head lolling slackly to the side.

A nauseatingly meaty flavor filled my mouth as the jolt of sudden energy faded away. I was starting to rack up a body count.

The Skullbreakers were adding to theirs too. I peeked out and saw Kai descending on one of their murderers, who was trying to make a run for it. Kai shoved him down and stood over him, ramming his heel into the guy's back, his eyes blazing with fury. My guys hadn't been able to carry out their plan to their satisfaction, but he still wasn't going to make this an easy death.

"You tried to take us down, but we're back," he snapped, shooting the guy's calf and then his groin. The man beneath him flailed and groaned. "This is what you get for screwing over the Skullbreakers. We don't die!"

He unloaded the rest of his bullets into the increasingly desperate body one by one, finishing with a shot to the skull, appropriately enough.

Nox charged into view, pummeling another of the guests of honor with an onslaught of crackling punches. The guy swayed and staggered, only held up by the momentum of the Skullbreakers boss's swings. His chest had already started to cave in with broken ribs.

"You aren't getting off," he snarled. "Time to pay for the twenty years we lost."

He cracked the guy's head open against the seat of the throne and roared for his recruits to surround the other three before they could dash off too.

Ruin leapt into view, delivering a flying kick that knocked another guest of honor onto the floor. He plunged a spatula that must have been with one of the platters into the man's chest like it was a knife and laughed in delight.

Jett dashed in with a flurry of smacks that appeared to rearrange the fourth man's entire body in an impossible formation that was not conducive to life. He didn't stop until the dickwad was twisted up like a human pretzel—one made by a not-particularly-skilled baker.

As Nox strode up to the last of their murderers, the balding guy fumbled with a gun it appeared he'd already emptied. Nox wrenched the balding guy's gun out of his hand and rammed the muzzle straight through the murderer's eye socket into his skull. I winced at the gruesome sight, but I couldn't say it wasn't fitting.

I'd lost track of the other Skullbreakers. There were still guns firing and minor wrestling matches commencing all around the room, although the activity was starting to quiet down. Mostly because there were probably more bodies lying limp on the floor than standing on their feet at this point.

When the shots and the other sounds of the fighting faded away completely, I crept out from under the table and picked my way through the bodies toward the throne. It looked like the few Skeleton Corps members who'd survived had decided they'd done enough damage and taken off.

Except for a greasy-haired man Ruin was looming over with a savage grin. The guy was hunched and shaking, clearly in the grips of supernaturally-inflicted terror.

"Please!" he was whimpering, clutching at Ruin's pantleg. "Don't hurt me. I swear I'll never do anything against you or your guys again. It wasn't even my idea. I just want to get out of here alive! Oh, God…"

I found it hard to have any sympathy. There was hardly anyone left *at all* in the Skeleton Corps's wake. It looked like my men had mostly survived because there'd been so many recruits who didn't have supernatural powers on their side taking bullets. A shudder ran through my body.

As we all gathered around Ruin, the man's gaze snagged on me. To my surprise, he lifted his hand to me next, his eyes widening with what looked like frantic hope. "The girl! You're with them—you can tell them to give me a break—I'll tell you where they have your sister."

I froze. "What?" I said, the bottom of my stomach dropping out.

"Your sister," the man babbled. "The kid. I—I can show you the last place they took her. I helped with the transport."

"How the fuck do you know anything about Lily's missing sister?" Nox growled, glaring down at the guy.

But he must be telling the truth, right? He shouldn't have known I had a sister or that she was missing unless he'd been involved.

The guy started trembling harder under Nox's glower. "I—I help out the bosses sometimes—they were doing it as a favor. Sometimes they do that. We do stuff for the big people in their tall towers, and they make sure the police stay off our backs and things like that. It wasn't *my* idea."

"Fuck!" Nox roared.

Kai's mouth had tensed into a pale line. He glanced at me. "The Gauntts have the Skeleton Corps in their pocket."

"Yeah," I said faintly. "I was putting those pieces together myself."

No wonder the Corps had ruled Mayfield so thoroughly until they'd been challenged by a bunch of guys with little sense of self-preservation, an intense need for revenge, and unexpected supernatural skills on their side. No wonder they'd attacked us tonight. The realization hit me with a jolt.

The words tumbled out. "They didn't double-double-cross you because they figured out your plan. They double-double-crossed you because you asked them to turn on the Gauntts." Which also explained why the marked boss hadn't shown up. Now that he'd wanted to go against their corporate benefactors, had his colleagues shut him up permanently so he couldn't make any waves?

That didn't matter right now. I yanked my mind back to the present. What mattered was all the deaths and the chaos had given both me and the guys what we'd wanted—their revenge, and my path to Marisol.

"Okay," I said to the Skeleton Corps guy. "You show us where my sister is, and we'll let you live. But if you're messing with us…"

"I'm not!" he insisted. "I swear. I'll take you there right now. We just need—"

A sudden shot blasted through the room. One of the men I'd assumed was dead had managed to lift his gun-hand to fire one last time. My heart lurched as my head whipped back toward the men gathered around me, afraid he'd shot our hostage before he could give me the answers I needed.

He hadn't. It was worse than that.

Ruin toppled back into the foot of the pinball machine, clutching his gut with blood bursting across his shirt like a miniature hurricane.

twenty-one

Lily

"Ruin!" I cried, leaping to his side. Just in that instant, his shirt looked twice as bloody as before. He sagged further, sliding down the pinball machine.

My entire focus narrowed down to the man in front of me, and the hum of my magic expanded until it was roaring in my ears alongside my pulse. I felt *his* pulse, pumping more blood out through the severed vessels as if it couldn't drain him fast enough.

Clammy fingers of panic squeezed around my gut. I did the only thing I could think of and shoved all the blood I could fix my energies on back into Ruin's body.

He came to a stop sitting on the floor, still leaning against the machine. I thrust out my hands, hovering them in front of the wound. And the stain spreading through his shirt… withdrew. It contracted on itself like the coffee marks on the packages I'd had to de-saturate weeks ago, but I wasn't moving the blood anywhere else in the room. I was pushing it into his body. Into the veins and possibly arteries torn along the bullet's path.

I couldn't heal him like this. I knew I wasn't doing anything but staving off the inevitable. But as long as I was guiding his blood through his body rather than out of it, he couldn't bleed to death. So I'd keep fucking staving as long as I could.

What would I do without Ruin's joyful exuberance? What would any of us do? Watching his head sway, it struck me abruptly how much he held our group of five together, smoothing out all the rough edges that might have jarred against each other without his presence.

We couldn't lose him. We just *couldn't*.

Jett and Kai dropped down on either side of their friend. I was vaguely aware of Nox striding across the room to the gunman who'd crumpled again. The bang of a gun—once, twice, three times—made me flinch, but I knew the Skullbreakers boss was only making sure the asswipe couldn't hurt anyone else.

If Ruin's attacker survived three bullets in his brain, then we had bigger problems.

"Hey," Kai said, snapping his fingers in front of Ruin's face. "Stay with us. You're not allowed to go anywhere."

Ruin looked at him blearily and managed—even now—a smile, as wobbly as it was. "Always so bossy," he mumbled. Then his gaze slid to me. His eyes sharpened. "You need to go get your sister. Some of the Skeleton guys ran. Might tell the Gauntts we're on to them. Need to get her before they move again."

The knowledge that he was right wrenched at me. "We have to get help for you first," I said through the roar of my magic.

"*No*," he insisted, waving a hand at me. "I've already died once. You need her."

"Ruin," Nox started.

The redhead swung his head to the side and narrowed his eyes at his boss. "Try to take me to a hospital instead of going for Lily's sister, and I'll tear the rest of my guts out myself."

I believed he'd make good on that threat. I bit my lip, and Kai pushed himself upright.

"Get him into Lily's car," he said, taking charge with his intellectual precision. "Between the three of us, we might be able to stabilize him *and* go after Marisol. Which is a better outcome than him committing seppuku by hand."

Nox muttered several swear words under his breath, but he motioned to Jett at the same time. He grabbed Ruin's shoulders as Jett hefted his feet. I kept all my attention trained on the flow of blood through Ruin's body—and making sure it stayed *in* that body.

"You too," Nox barked at the shivering Skeleton Corps guy, whose supernaturally-driven fearfulness hadn't faltered yet. "If *you* want to live, you'd better get us to her sister—fast."

The dope scrambled after us. We hustled out, me fumbling for the keys in my distraction, and piled into Fred 2.0 in a literal heap. Well, Nox snatched the keys when I tossed them to him and got into the front next to our guide, but Kai, Jett, and I squeezed into the back while laying Ruin across us on Kai's brisk instructions.

As Nox gunned the engine and the Corps guy started mumbling hasty directions, I stroked Ruin's bright hair, trying not to let the ache of worry in my stomach overwhelm my focus. He beamed up at me, but with a glazed quality to his eyes that only deepened the ache.

Kai nudged his glasses up his nose where he sat at the other end of the seat under Ruin's partly folded legs. "All right. I'm fairly familiar with the structures of the typical internal organs."

"Of course you are," Jett muttered.

Kai glowered at him. "Be thankful for it. *You* get to be the star of this show, though. You can change the shape of things—that means you should be able to adjust the shape of the pieces of Ruin that got broken so they're not so broken anymore."

Jett's jaw went slack. "You want me to—to perform *surgery* on him? With *magic*?"

"Do you have any better ideas?" Kai snapped. "Now let's get on with it before Lily bursts her own heart with all the effort she's putting into picking up our slack."

A dribble of moisture ran down my forehead and over my nose. I hadn't even noticed I was sweating before that moment. It wasn't just my stomach aching. A dull throbbing was creeping all through my nerves.

He was right. Maybe not about my heart specifically, but I was wearing myself out way faster than I liked.

I couldn't stop. Ruin needed me.

Kai leaned over and peeled up Ruin's shirt. "We have to see what we're dealing with. In that area, the bullet probably ruptured an intestine as well as a bunch of veins, maybe even an artery... Can you use your superpower to feel out what's already there just sticking your hand over it?"

"Yeah," Jett said, his voice a bit ragged and his face turning queasily green. He set his hand over the wound. "I think I can do that. But I don't want to piece the wrong parts together."

"Go in as far as you can reach into the flesh with your energy and see if you can sense a sort of bloody tube slanting on the diagonal downward. And if there are any breaks in it."

"There are," I said faintly. With Kai's description, my own awareness of the liquid I was manipulating—and the passages I was manipulating it through—got clearer. "There's one hole on the side where most of the blood is trying to escape. I think the bullet must have scraped across it on the way through."

"Fuck," Jett muttered, and closed his eyes. "Let me try. I don't know how well this will work."

"You can make a guy's nose grow to five times its

normal size," Kai pointed out. "I think you can stretch a little arterial wall to fill in a bullet hole."

Jett bit his lip. His hand flexed against Ruin's broken flesh. And ever so slowly I felt the pressure of the blood that'd been pushing to get past my hold ebbing.

"You're doing it!" I said. "It's getting sealed up."

Jett drew in a shaky breath and continued his work, with Kai talking him through the levels of veins and intestines and muscles. Finally, the artist slumped back against the seat, all the color drained from his face, as if he was the one who'd been bleeding out. "I can't do any more. Not right now. I feel like *my* body's about to split apart."

Sometime during our efforts, Ruin had slipped into unconsciousness. Maybe that was for the best. I wasn't sure how much Jett's efforts might have hurt. He was breathing steadily. When I withdrew the energy I'd been sending into his body with a rush of relief, only a little more blood seeped out through the still-open bullet wound.

"That'll do for now," Kai said.

I swiped my sleeve across my forehead and glanced across the car at him. His expression was tight, his eyes gone hard, but I didn't think it was with lack of emotion. It was the opposite. He was shaken by Ruin's injury too.

"If it's not enough," I forced myself to ask, "if his body fails... could he find another one, like you all did the first time?"

Kai rubbed his mouth. "I don't know. I didn't even know we could definitely manage it the first time. I have no idea what the rules might be—whether our spirits might only be capable of it once, whether it makes a difference that theoretically we've avenged ourselves now so we don't have that factor holding us in the world of the living…" He exhaled with a rasp of frustration. "I'd rather not lose him and have to find out."

"Of course." I stroked Ruin's hair again, my gut twisting.

I'd been so fixated on him that I hadn't been paying attention to the guys up front. Abruptly, the Skeleton Corps dude stiffened in his seat. Then he lunged at Nox as if to grab the steering wheel.

Nox fended him off with a slap that sent the guy reeling in the opposite direction and hollered, "A little help here?"

Thankfully, Kai was right behind the dickhead. He leaned forward to swat him. "Keep quiet and point us the rest of the way to where Lily's sister is being held."

Ruin's emotional influence had obviously worn off. Kai couldn't force the guy to answer questions, but the command he had given clearly worked. Though the dipshit scowled the whole time, his hand jerked up whenever Nox needed to make a turn.

While we'd scrambled to help Ruin, Fred 2.0 had taken us most of the way out of the city. We passed the last of the tightly-packed buildings and rumbled on into the countryside, where the night swallowed most of our surroundings beyond the sporadic streetlamps along the highway.

I'd already guessed that the Gauntts had taken Marisol beyond the city limits, but a chill crept over me as we zoomed on through the darkness. Just how far away was she? And what were we going to face when we got there?

After a couple more turns, a dank odor crept through the car's ventilation that made my nose wrinkle. It smelled like… manure.

Most likely, it was manure. The Skeleton Corps dude pointed us down a bumpy dirt track that led to a spread of large farm buildings. There were several barns, two silos, and a big cement building I couldn't have labeled. A few lights were on around the outskirts of that building. From one of the barns, a disgruntled moo carried through the air.

As we parked near a couple of other vehicles already there, two men came out of the cement building to see what was up. A light over the door blinked on, illuminating them and making them squint at us through the dark.

Kai smacked our guide's shoulder. "Keep your mouth shut and don't do anything except bring the girl here."

The guy got out of the car. The men by the building clearly recognized him, because one of them nodded and called out a greeting. Following Kai's orders, the first guy said nothing and simply marched past them into the building. They shot puzzled looks at him and the car, and one of them headed in after him.

Raised voices carried from inside. Nox readied his gun and glanced back at the others. "We may need to do a little more laying down of the law. Get ready."

Even as he said the words, the guy strode back into view, tugging Marisol with him. My heart leapt to my throat. She was still wearing her pajamas, which were wrinkled and drooping now, although someone had given her a pair of grimy sneakers. Her head whipped to one side and the other, her eyes wide with confusion.

A few other men had gathered around our dope, demanding to know what was going on. One of them grasped his arm.

That seemed to be the Skullbreakers' cue. They shoved the car doors open. Nox sprang out, shooting two guys before his feet had even planted firmly on the ground. Kai and Jett squirmed out from under Ruin as gingerly as they could and dashed into the fray.

Murmuring a pained apology to Ruin, I laid his head down on the seat and heaved myself out too.

More men charged out of the concrete building, but not many. It wasn't anything like the crazed battle in the restaurant. The Skullbreakers picked them all off, charging around them so they could fire without risking Marisol.

That didn't mean my sister was having an easy time of it, though. She shrieked and ducked down, squeezing her arms around her knees. Her whole body shook as if

EVA CHASE

she were in the grips of one of Ruin's supernaturally inflicted terrors.

The second the way was clear, I dashed over to her and knelt beside her, gripping her shoulder. "It's okay now, Mare. No one can hurt you now. I'm here. We're getting you home."

Her head jerked up, and I immediately knew it wasn't going to be that easy. Defiance flashed in her eyes.

"No!" she screamed, shoving away from me. "Get away from me!"

The Gauntts were still working their influence on her, making her terrified of *me*. She darted away across the farmyard, and I bolted after her.

I had to break the spell. That was the only way to bring her home properly. I couldn't stand to drive her all the way back to the apartment with her thinking she'd been captured by the enemy for some horrible doom.

I pelted across the hard-packed dirt as fast as I could go. Marisol wasn't any slouch, but she'd probably been sitting for most of the time she'd been in the Gauntts' custody. Her legs weren't up to a marathon. They wobbled under her as she veered toward one of the barns, and I caught her right by the door, wrapping my fingers around her upper arm.

"No, no!" she squealed, trying to slap me away. "I hate you."

I let the words bounce off me. They weren't her— they were only the garbage the Gauntts were pumping into her brain with their magic.

My nerves were frayed from helping Ruin, but from deep down inside me I hauled up one last surge of my marshy magic. With all my remaining strength, I threw it against the mark I could sense on her flesh.

I still had to batter it two times. But the second time, the crack of the mark shattering reverberated through my entire body.

Marisol gasped, and her arm went limp in my grasp. "Lily?" she said in a tiny voice. "I—oh my *God*."

The last word broke off with a sob. I gathered her in my arms and hugged her, and after a few seconds she squeezed me back even harder.

It would have been a perfect reunion if another car hadn't growled into view right then.

I lifted my head, eyeing the vehicle as it came to a stop off to the side of the lane. It didn't fit with the other cars already at the farm. Too big, too sleek, too posh. A tremor of apprehension ran through me.

"Come on, Mare," I murmured. "Let's get you out of here. You can even ride shotgun."

The guys had gathered around my car. They formed a human shield for me and Marisol as I hurried her over.

The posh car's doors opened, and four figures stepped out. Not just Nolan and Marie Gauntt, but Thomas and Olivia, their younger counterparts, too. My teeth clenched. So the younger generation was in on this psychotic scheme as well.

Nox didn't hesitate. He fired a shot at the Gauntts immediately, aiming at Marie's head over the top of her still open door. But her hand shot up and her mouth twitched, and energy quivered through the air. I watched in horror as the bullet pinged off some sort of invisible wall and plunked to the ground instead.

"Get in the car!" I shouted. I didn't want to wait around and see what other magic these monsters could throw at us. I had Marisol back, and I intended for us all to make it out of here alive, no matter what we had to deal with later.

Nox huffed but dropped into the driver's seat. He started the ignition while keeping his eyes and his pistol trained on the Gauntts. I pushed Marisol into the passenger seat, where she curled up with a shell-shocked expression, and darted around to the back with Nox covering me. Kai and Jett were squirming in beneath Ruin's prone body.

Nolan Gauntt stepped forward as I moved. He raised his hand too. "I'm afraid this ends here," he said, and started to twist his wrist.

Fear jolted through my chest, and the hum ripped through me from depths I hadn't even known I had in me.

"It ends for you!" I yelled, and whipped my power at him on instinct alone.

I felt the rush of blood through his bulky body and slammed it toward his heart in one urgent push. Nolan's arm faltered, and he staggered on his feet. The walls of his heart strained, the muscles fraying but not quite bursting.

The other Gauntts jostled around him, and more

unnerving electricity laced the air. They were trying to fend off my attack. But I'd already gotten my grasp on him. I'd used up so much energy already, but if I could just hold on a little longer, wrench at him a little more…

Jett let out a yelp from the back seat. My gaze jerked over in time to see blood spurting from Ruin's wound. Our quick fix had been a little too temporary.

For a split-second, it felt as if the entire world hung in the balance. Nolan had fallen to his knees, wheezing. Marie had crouched to his side with a cry. Olivia and Thomas were marching toward me, a blast of energy hitting me across the head and making my mind spin. My thoughts narrowed down to one question.

Did I want this night to end in death or life?

It was only a question for another split-second after that. Then I was diving into the car, whipping my concentration back to saving one of the men I loved.

Nox hit the gas and tore backward over the dirt road so fast I was almost jostled back out the still-open door behind me. Ruin shuddered and gasped. Whatever the Gauntts threw at us as we fled, it made the engine groan and the metal frame shriek.

But they either weren't powerful enough to deal with us while we were speeding away from them, or they were too distracted by their fallen patriarch. Nox swung the car around, and we careened away into the night, leaving them far behind.

I leaned over and willed the blood back into Ruin's body while Kai and Jett spat hasty directions and observations back and forth. And somewhere in there, Ruin opened his eyes.

"Isn't anyone going to close that door?" he said, knitting his brow. "I like the breeze, but it seems kind of dangerous for Lily."

And that was when I knew for sure I'd chosen right.

twenty-two

Jett

Ruin would not shut up. That was nothing new, but you'd think a near-fatal gunshot wound would at least simmer the guy down a little.

"Oh, I love this show!" he exclaimed from where we'd set him up invalid-style on the apartment's sofa, sprawled out across the cushions with his head propped up and a blanket wrapped around him. Lily had even pushed the TV stand over so he could flip through the channels without having to crane his neck.

He was waving the remote at it now. "They *think* they're all in the afterlife, but really—"

"Hey!" Lily interrupted, hustling over. "Stay still. You don't want to burst your stitches."

He looked at her slightly mournfully before a renewed smile sprang across his face. "You're so good at taking care of me, Angelfish. I can't wait until I can take care of *you* again, too."

Lily sputtered a cough, her gaze darting to where her little sister was sitting at the dining table. Marisol's head was still drooped after the long talk, interspersed with many hugs and a few tears, that they'd had while the doctor Kai had tracked down had patched up my own attempt at bodily patchwork on Ruin. Or, the guy had seemed like some kind of medical person. From the amount of little hairs clinging to his lab coat, he might have actually been a veterinarian.

But then, Ruin could definitely be an animal. Hardy har har.

In any case, the guy had known enough about the human body to mutter several times that it was a shock Ruin was even still alive. We hadn't mentioned the magical component to that fact. There'd been a lot of slathering of antibiotic gels as well as plenty of stitching, to the point that I suspected even Ruin's stitches had stitches.

The doctor had left a bottle of foamy pink stuff that was supposed to sanitize Ruin from the inside out or something. Lily had stuck it in the fridge before Mr. Enthusiasm could down the whole thing in one go. Ruin was settling for gnawing on his favorite spicy jerky until it was time for his next dose. None of us were sure that eating anything, let alone the kind of stuff that'd burn your tongue off, was a good idea, but we were a little afraid of what he might try to do if we didn't at least allow him that small indulgence.

The guy annoyed me sometimes, but I couldn't imagine running with the Skullbreakers without him. We'd be a depressingly dour bunch, wouldn't we? I might value my grim moods for the creative flow they often got me into, but that didn't mean I wanted my surroundings to be equally somber 24-7.

Marisol didn't look fazed by Ruin's suggestive remark, if she'd even processed it. Lily bobbed down to give Ruin a quick peck on the cheek and then went back to her sister. "Do you want anything to eat?" I heard her murmuring. "Or you could get to bed. It is pretty late."

Marisol shuddered. "No," she said quickly. "When I close my eyes and let my mind drift, all that stuff comes back to me even more. I'll just—I'll watch some TV with Ruin."

She pulled her chair over to the living room area and shot our human-shaped beam of sunshine a cautious smile. Ruin, of course, grinned back at her. She'd only been introduced to us a couple of hours ago, but naturally he was already her favorite.

Kai was standing by the kitchen doorway, skimming through something on his phone. Nox took in the scene in the apartment and started stalking back and forth from one end of the main room to the other. The floor creaked faintly under his increasingly massive frame. It was hard to believe that body had once belonged to a professor with an entirely mediocre physique.

"It almost happened again," the boss growled abruptly, slamming his hand into his fist. He stopped by the dining room table, glancing at Ruin and then at the rest of us. "I fucked up and let you down again."

He spoke low enough not to disturb Ruin and Marisol on the other side of the room, but the frustration and anguish rippling through his voice was unmistakable.

Lily frowned and stepped closer to him. "What are you talking about? You didn't screw anything up."

"I did," he said, his hands now flexing at his sides like he needed something bigger to punch. "I fucked up twenty years ago by not cracking down on the fucking Silver Scythes hard enough, which meant they felt bold enough to go off inciting the Skeleton Corps pricks, and then I fucked up tonight not realizing the goddamned Corps was going to turn on us again. How many of our recruits kicked the bucket? *Ruin* almost kicked it!"

"We got our revenge," Kai pointed out, but with unusual hesitance.

Nox's eyes flashed. "Yes. We managed that one thing. But it would mean fuck-all if we died all over again in the process. And who the hell knows if we've finally put the fear of us into the Skeleton Corps or if they'll be after us again now that the truce is totally dead. They've got the Gauntts jerking their chains, so they probably won't back down. It's a fucking mess."

I couldn't dispute that. There was a hollow sensation in the pit of my stomach if I let myself try to think beyond the next hour or so, to contemplate what trials we'd have to get through next. But he was wrong in the other direction, about that first event. So fucking wrong.

The familiar guilt wound through my torso again, constricting around my guts and then my lungs. But how the hell could I just stand here while the best friend I'd ever had, the only boss I'd ever been happy to take orders from, beat himself up over *my* failings?

I opened my mouth and closed it again. I'd been holding the story in so long it felt like a bowling ball I was trying to shove up my throat.

"That's not your fault," Lily was saying. "None of us realized the Skeleton Corps were planning a double-double-cross or whatever you'd call it. Not even Kai, and he's supposed to know everything."

Seeing the compassion on her face just about killed me all over again. I wanted to grab her in my arms and drown myself in her scent like I hadn't let myself do until just a few nights ago, as if I could escape the sins of my past that way.

I'd only discovered just how good things could really be with her in every way, how coming together with her bodily woke up something *more* in me rather than making what we had between us less extraordinary. After she heard this, would I ever get the chance to touch her like that again?

Kai had made a face. "I'm not quite clairvoyant. But it's true that I should have been keeping a closer eye on activities outside the clubhouse."

"I ordered you to keep an eye on the assholes *in* the clubhouse," Nox retorted. "I'm the boss, it was my call, just like everything the first time around—"

My voice finally launched from my throat. "No, it wasn't."

All three of them jerked around to stare at me. An unwelcome warmth crept across my face, but I forced myself to keep talking, hoping the momentum would stop me from stalling out before I got to the important parts.

"I was the last one to get to our real clubhouse the night the Skeleton Corps came after us the first time," I said. "You remember? I was driving slow on my bike because the pattern of the stars was giving me an idea for a painting or something like that. I don't remember exactly. But there was this guy skulking around near the building, watching it and making notes on his phone."

Kai frowned. "You never mentioned that."

"I thought I'd dealt with it," I said. "And then I got distracted by whatever you all were talking about when I came in. It didn't seem like an emergency. I roared right over to the guy, and he pulled a gun on me. I was pissed off that he was spying on us and waving shit at me so I ran the fucking bike right into him. Then I got off and fucked him up some more before tossing him in the ditch. It was already dark. I figured we'd get around to burying him sometime later that night."

"What does this have to do with the attack?" Nox demanded.

The intensity in his gaze made me want to shrink into myself, but I managed to keep going. "He wasn't dead when I left him. I was *sure* he was almost there, he had to be dy*ing*, but he still—the blood was trickling out of him into the puddles in the ditch, and his breath was leaving with this perfect rattle, and it was like a masterpiece, the way it all came together... and I couldn't bring myself to break it. It was too good. I wanted my last experience of the moment to be like that."

I glanced at the floor and swallowed hard. Even knowing what'd come after, even with Lily staring at me along with the others—Lily who got squeamish even killing a guy who was trying to do the same to her in that moment—the awe of the scene I'd created all those years ago still lit me up like a candle.

But it'd been garbage, not art. It'd been garbage, because—

"He mustn't have died," I said hoarsely. "At least not soon enough. He must have had enough life left to get in touch with the rest of his crew, and when they came racing over it wasn't a scouting anymore but retribution. If I'd finished the job properly instead of making something pretty, we wouldn't have been killed. It was *my* fuck-up, not yours."

I braced myself—I didn't know what for. I had no idea what to expect in response to my confession. I'd probably have deserved it if Nox had torn me apart, not just for my pretentious selfishness but for lying by omission all these years. Acting like I hadn't had any idea that anyone was gunning for us.

"If you knew it was the Skeleton Corps—" Kai started.

I shook my head with a snap. "I didn't. I had no clue who the dude was. He didn't have any insignia—I didn't even know he was part of a crew rather than some random asshole with a private agenda. But it was at least a fifty-fifty chance. I should have offed him before I walked away. I should have gotten us out there to take care of him the second I met up with you."

I couldn't remember what the other guys had been talking about, only that they'd been laughing and bouncing ideas back and forth with eager exhilaration. I'd been hyped up from making my bloody art, and in that moment, dealing with the body had felt like something that could wait. A chore I didn't want to bring us all down for until it was absolutely necessary.

So fucking stupid. I hadn't really known how much any of this mattered back then, had I?

Nox was still staring at me. "Fucking hell, Jett," he said finally. "Why didn't you say anything before?"

I shrugged. "You know how it was when we were dead—everything was so woozy, and then after... I didn't see how it'd do any good to bring it up, since it'd already happened, and I didn't know anything that could help with our revenge. We were finally *back*, and I didn't want to fuck that up by giving all of you a reason to hate my guts." So really, that decision had been utterly selfish too.

"Man," Nox said, exhaling in a ragged rush, and then he did the last thing I'd ever have expected. He walked over to me and yanked me into a one-armed hug.

He wasn't Ruin, so it remained just one arm, and it only lasted about two seconds, keeping his manly macho status intact. But I couldn't say Nox had *ever* hugged me before. I blinked at him as he drew back, totally bewildered. Had that been some kind of revenge hug where I would suddenly realize he'd stabbed a knife into my back in the process?

But all my internal organs felt to still be in working order, and Nox was cuffing my shoulder now, not quite hard enough to really hurt.

"That story is so fucking *you*," he said. "Making a masterpiece out of some jerk you ran over. We didn't even have anyone posted keeping watch to catch the pricks. We were all something back then, weren't we? Out of our fucking minds. Kings of Lovell Rise, but that wasn't hard to pull off. This time—this time we're doing it right. We know how to really rule."

It took me a second to reel in my jaw. "You're not pissed?"

"Of course I'm pissed," he said in his usual cocky tone. "But I also know that we've all been idiots plenty of times, and your fuck-up doesn't change the fact that I fucked up too, and—we're here now. We got our second chance. What's the point if we're going to sit around sulking about how we screwed up the first one? We have to make sure we keep *this* one."

I agreed with him, but I couldn't quite believe that I was getting off this easy. I glanced at Kai, whose mouth twisted into a thin smirk.

"I didn't fuck up to that extent," he said. "But I sure as hell wasn't keeping a close enough eye on things back then. And you know what? I like this second chance better than the first one anyway. We've got magic; we've got Lily. We got our revenge tonight. We're going to make this entire goddamn city our masterpiece."

Lily let out a soft laugh under her breath. "I'd like to see that."

So would I. A thrill tingled through me at his words, and suddenly I wanted to hug all of them, which was even more bizarre than Nox getting cuddly. "I guess I should tell Ruin too," I said awkwardly.

Nox waved the suggestion off. "He'll probably be overjoyed to hear it. Tell him whenever you feel like it, but I don't think you need to worry about *his* reaction."

I looked at the guy on the couch, chortling away at the actors on the screen as if his insides weren't currently held together with thread and shoddy surgical magic, and had to admit that our boss was right about that too.

Lily's sister let out a small laugh too, and a hint of a smile crossed Lily's weary face. "I think—" she started.

A frenetic beeping cut her off, emanating from Kai's laptop where he'd left it on the coffee table. He dashed over and snatched it up, flipping it open as he did. His face lit up with what I could only describe as maniacal enthusiasm.

"It's the motion sensors out by the Gauntts' favorite spot in the marsh," he announced, gazing around at the rest of us. "Someone's out there right now."

twenty-three

Lily

At Kai's declaration, my pulse stuttered. I reined myself in. "It could be anyone, couldn't it? A bunch of teenagers partying out by the water or some tramp wandering around."

Kai's eyes gleamed behind his glasses with manic intensity. "Possible, yes. Likely, no. There are a lot of stretches of the marsh that are closer to any given town if a bunch of punks wanted to splash around and throw beer bottles into the reeds. And it's not ideal stomping grounds for someone looking for shelter for the night. And you *did* just bring Nolan Gauntt to his knees."

"I didn't kill him," I said. "I *couldn't*."

Nox had straightened up with renewed alertness. "You gave him a good punch in the heart, though, didn't you? That has to have left some damage. Maybe they're out there working some magic to heal him up like we did for Ruin."

"They won't do half as good a job as you all did," Ruin informed us with typical cheer, and then winced. He might have been pieced back together, but the pieces weren't exactly in prime condition.

Marisol had turned in her chair, her eyes wide. "If they're out at that spot you think is special, doing some ritual or whatever all they do—does that mean they could mess with my head again? Make me go back to them?"

The quaver that rippled through her voice and the way her knuckles whitened where she clutched the back of the chair brought a lump into my throat that almost choked me.

"No," I reassured her as emphatically as I could, going over to wrap my arm around her shoulder. "I took the mark off you. I broke their hold. They can't get at you again."

Not from afar, anyway. There were physical means a person could use to capture someone, and then who was to say they couldn't mark her all over again? I'd been thirteen when Nolan had done it to me. There might not be any age cut-off at all—they just happened to prefer groping and manipulating kids.

Which was why we couldn't ignore this.

"We should go out there," I said to Nox, my voice coming out quiet and strained. "If he's weak, we should take them down while we have the chance. Or at least we'd get the opportunity to figure out more about their magic so we can get the better of them when we're more equipped to do it." My gaze darted back to my sister. "But I can't leave Marisol."

"If we want a chance of destroying them tonight, we need you there, Siren," Nox said. "You're the one who nearly did him in to begin with. I can punch 'em around a little, but that won't do much if they can deflect actual bullets, and Kai and Jett have to touch 'em to work their powers."

"I'll be here with your sister," Ruin pointed out brightly, as if he was the more capable one between the two of them. If a bunch of bad guys came charging in here, Marisol would have to be the one defending *him*.

"No offense, friend, but I think she could use at least a little backup that can kick butt without tearing themselves open," Kai said matter-of-factly. He turned to Nox. "There were a few of the new recruits who held their own against the Skeleton Corps. We could ask them to play bodyguards. They've passed a bigger test than we could invent on our own."

"If they even want to side with us after that bloodbath," Jett muttered.

Nox huffed. "We did technically win. And there's no reason a sixteen-year-old can't learn how to defend herself damn well too." He nodded to Marisol. "I was fourteen when I first got my hands on a gun. You think you can handle one?"

"Um," I said, feeling like this conversation was spiraling out of control in a direction I'd never have intended, but the eager light that came into my sister's face stopped me. She raised her chin with a more determined expression than I'd ever seen from her.

"Hell, yes," she said. "I want to be able to blast those assholes away if they come after me again."

Well, in that case, who was I to argue? I opened and closed my mouth a few times as if that might jog loose a reasonable objection and settled on staying silent.

As Kai started making calls to the surviving Skullbreakers recruits, Nox strode into the guys' bedroom and came back with another pistol, a smaller one than his usual.

"Here," he said, motioning for Marisol to stand up. She lifted her hands, and he showed her how to grasp the grip.

"Keep your index finger off the trigger unless you're about to shoot," he told her. "It's too easy to squeeze instinctively if you get startled. Since you're a newbie, you'll want to steady it with your other hand. There'll still be pretty bad recoil when you fire it, since you're not used to that. If you need to shoot someone, aim for their chest. You're likely to hit something that'll at least slow them down, and it's harder to miss than trying for a head shot."

Marisol lifted the gun tentatively, pointing it at the bare wall, and practiced steadying it the way he'd shown her. Nox pointed to her feet. "If you have the chance to prepare yourself, it's better if you have one foot a little ahead of the other for balance. And keep your muscles as loose as possible, even if you're scared."

I'd never thought I'd want to see my sister learning how to use a gun. I still wasn't overjoyed that she needed to. But at the same time, watching the Skullbreakers boss coach her with so much confidence in her abilities sent a tingle through me.

I still wasn't totally sure how to explain to her about our odd relationship and how it'd come into being, but it already felt like we were all family.

"You good?" Nox asked, eyeing Marisol. "Ideally, we'd find a place to do some trial shots and all that, but we've got to head out. Tomorrow I can take you through more of the paces."

My sister's expression hardened with even more determination. "I'll do what I have to do. I hope I *do* get the chance to shoot him."

I didn't have to ask who she meant. My throat constricted. As she lowered the gun, I wrapped her in a tight hug. "If I have anything to say about it, no one's going to bother you at all. But don't be afraid to protect yourself if you need to."

She nodded. As I withdrew, Kai was just finishing up one last phone call. "I'm not having anyone come into the apartment," he said. "I'm sure you'd rather not have total strangers hovering around. We've got one guy outside the apartment door, two in the lobby, and two more outside the building, keeping watch. If they see any reason for concern, they'll let us know and take action."

I sucked in a breath. That was about as good as I could hope for. I bent down and gave Ruin a quick but emphatic kiss, trying not to let myself think about the fact that this could be the last time I got to do it. "We're going to give them hell for you."

He grinned back at me. "And plenty for you too. All the hell."

My lips twitched with bittersweet amusement. "All the hell."

There wasn't time for anything else, not if we wanted to have a chance to get to the marsh while the Gauntts were still present. We rushed out of the apartment, where a recruit fearsome-looking enough to reassure me a little was standing in the hall, and dashed down to my car.

Nox still had my keys, and I didn't argue when he got into the driver's seat. I'd imagine he had way more experience at high-speed driving than I did. Kai got into the passenger seat muttering instructions, so Jett and I ended up in the back again.

For all my efforts to keep Ruin's blood inside his body, there were still some damp streaks on the seat. I ended up sitting in the middle to avoid the worst of them, cringing inwardly and sending up another prayer to whatever powers might be that the sweetest of us would make it through tonight all right.

As the car took off down the street, my shoulder jostled against Jett's. I was so used to his previous aversion to physical contact that I tensed up, but a second later, his hand had wrapped around mine.

"We'll get through this," he said quietly, under Nox and Kai's hasty back-and-forth. "If for no other reason than because I had my head up my ass for too long and I haven't gotten anywhere near enough time to enjoy being with you."

The declaration from a guy who was usually so sparing with words made my heart ache in a way I didn't mind at all. My thoughts leapt back to his anguished confession, the guilt he'd obviously been holding on to for so long that explained so much about him I hadn't understood before.

The fact that he'd felt so guilty about it only proved how much he cared for the guys he'd thrown his lot in with. Maybe his brutally artistic outlook wasn't exactly typical or totally sane, but I knew he was there for them and for me in every way that mattered.

I tipped my head against Jett's, breathing in the tart scent of paint that clung to him even after everything we'd been through today, and squeezed his hand. "Good. Because I haven't gotten anywhere near enough of you either."

Of any of them, really. Wouldn't it be something if we could have a week or a month or, hell, a year of normal life as the family I'd gotten a glimpse of back in the apartment?

Relatively normal, of course. The guys were never going to be *normal* normal, and probably I wouldn't either. But something less chaotic and murder-y than this should definitely be possible.

We whipped through the city and out past Lovell Rise, so fast the tires felt as if they'd lifted right off the road at times. There wasn't much traffic this late at night, and once we were out of the city, Nox switched off the headlights to avoid drawing notice. We got out to the fields around the marsh in half the time it should have taken.

As we came closer to the spit where we'd set up the motion detectors, Nox slowed. Kai told him exactly where to stop, where he judged we were still far enough away that anyone at the edge of the water wouldn't be able to hear the engine yet. The road had just about ended anyway. Then we scrambled out and slunk across the fields, squinting through the darkness for any lights or signs of movement.

What if we'd missed them? What if they were already gone, and we'd come out here for nothing? Those questions gripped my chest as we treaded over the matted grass. My heart was thumping so loud I was a little afraid that our targets would hear *that* even if they hadn't picked up on the car.

We were just coming to a patch of trees that hid the last short stretch of dry land before the marsh began when hushed voices reached our ears from up ahead. We hadn't seen any other cars around, and no roads reached this far anyway. Had the Gauntts parked on one of the other lanes a mile or more away and walked the rest of the distance?

We eased to the side so the trees would cover our approach and crept closer. Once we reached the cluster of saplings, we peered between them toward the spit.

We hadn't missed the Gauntts at all. In fact, there were more of them here than I'd expected. Six figures stood out by the far end of the spit, vague in the moonlight. Two of them were clearly children, their frames gawky and their heads only coming up to the shoulders of the taller adults around them.

Whatever the family was up to, it looked like they'd brought Nolan and Marie Junior too.

We weren't close enough for me to make out any of the words they said, but a rapid chorus of murmurs was spilling out into the air with a dissonant rhythm that made the hairs on the back of my arms rise. The largest, broadest figure, whose face I briefly made out as the original Nolan's, had been held up between his wife and his son, his frame sagging. As we watched, they guided him forward... and lowered him down into the shallow water at the edge of the spit.

twenty-four

Lily

Nox glanced over at the rest of us, the slivers of moonlight that filtered through the saplings' scrawny branches catching on the whites of his eyes. He widened them as if to say, *What the fuck are they doing?*

Kai spread his hands in a gesture of confusion. I shook my head. Jett shrugged.

Nox frowned and then made a small motion with his hand for us to move closer.

The water lapped around Nolan's body, with a faint splash as he—or his family—pushed him farther into it. We bent down and crawled closer on our hands and knees. The guys might have felt like they were spies or super soldiers carrying out a dangerous mission. *I felt* like I'd been warped back into my childhood games of pretend. The pebbles lodged in the damp ground bit into my skin through my tights. I hiked my dress up so it wouldn't make any noise dragging across the grass.

I was definitely never wearing this outfit again.

We stopped by the cattails that choked the water at the foot of the spit. The Gauntts were still some twenty feet away by its tip, so focused on whatever they were doing with their murmuring and their impromptu bathing session that they hadn't noticed our arrival. We crouched there, peering through the swaying reeds and listening now that their voices had come into sharper focus.

At least they were giving Nolan Senior his bath on the side of the spit closer to us, where we could see reasonably well... even if we had no idea what we were really looking at.

At first, their words sounded as incomprehensible as they had when we'd been farther away. Maybe I hadn't been able to make anything out because they were using another language—or none at all—not because of the distance?

A soft thump near my foot made me flinch, but it was only a frog hopping over to join me. A few more amphibious friends plopped into place around us like some kind of squishy green bodyguards. Somehow I didn't think they'd be much help if the Gauntts discovered us here, but I appreciated the marsh's vote of support all the same.

I leaned closer, straining my ears. Most of the things

the Gauntts were saying seemed to be nonsense words, but here and there I caught a few I recognized. Someone said something about "life and death," and someone else talked about "rejuvenating waters." The three adults still on the land started swinging their hands up and down like they were doing the wave at a ballgame.

The posturing looked ridiculous, but it was accomplishing something. A quiver of energy raced through the air, prickling over my skin. It intensified until I could feel it tingling through my body all the way down to my bones.

What the hell were they doing?

Something for Nolan's benefit, presumably. His breath rattled as he lay there, submerged in the murky water with only his face and a sliver of his chest showing. The gasps for air were coming farther apart than when we'd first arrived.

I'd really done a number on him. Unfortunately, it looked like they had some plan for reviving him.

I gritted my teeth and glanced toward my guys. Should we jump in and interrupt, to try to finish what I'd started? The supernatural power resonating through the air made me nervous. I didn't know how the Gauntts might have protected themselves already, how much they might be able to throw at us here.

This time, we didn't have a getaway method right next to us. If we showed our hand at the wrong moment, it could be a death sentence for both us and the people we'd left back home.

Nox caught my gaze and grimaced. He nudged Kai

lightly with his shoulder. Kai studied the figures on the spit for several seconds longer and then shook his head.

"We wait," he said under his breath, so soft the words blended into the breeze. I could only hear him because I was so close. "Whatever they're doing, it appears to be taking a lot out of them. When they're leaving, they'll have exhausted all that energy, and we'll be more rested."

His reasoning made sense. Jett inclined his head in agreement, but he'd taken out his gun, resting it in his hand on the muddy ground in front of him. I reached into myself and focused on the hum of energy I could easily provoke with the Gauntts in my sights. I needed to be prepared to go on the attack—or the defensive—in an instant.

The Gauntts clustered closer around this side of the end of the spit. Well, most of them did. The girl stood rigidly in the same place she'd been all along, now a few feet away from the others. The boy, the grownups ushered to the edge of the solid ground and pushed into the water alongside his namesake.

He didn't look as if he went as willingly as his grandfather had. His limbs twitched as the water, which must have been uncomfortably chilly, washed over them, and his head jerked briefly to the side. But the adults kept up their bizarre murmuring, and Olivia—his mother—prodded him farther into the marsh. He bobbed among the reeds, looking as stiff as his sister, just horizontal rather than vertical.

The whole scene had already been creepy, but now a

more potent tendril of apprehension coiled around my stomach. Abruptly I was sure that whatever they were going to do, it was going to be more horrible than anything I'd seen from them before.

The three adults still on the land knelt down along the bank of the spit. They lowered their hands into the water on either side of the Nolans' heads, Thomas in the middle between his father and his son, Olivia at her father's—father in law's?—other side, Marie next to her grandson. A tremor ran through their hunched bodies.

They kept murmuring, scooping water with their hands and pouring it over the mostly-submerged figures. The vibration of ominous energy in the air thickened even more. I sucked my lower lip under my teeth and nearly bit right through it.

I wanted to reach out to the water of the marsh and tell it to stop this. To ignore whatever they were calling on it to do. But I knew how to bend it to my will, not how to convince it to shun anyone else. And the Gauntts knew about my watery powers. The second I tossed a wave or a torrent at them, they'd know I was here.

They were pouring marsh water over the Nolans' faces now. Nolan Senior made no sound other than a faint hitch of his ragged breath. Nolan Junior briefly sputtered and squirmed. My legs ached to run in there and drag him out of the marsh—but then I'd be trading his comfort for my life and my men's and even my sister's. I clenched my hands, my fingernails digging into my palms.

All at once, Thomas and Olivia shoved down on the older man. He plunged right under the water, probably all the way to the shallow bottom. As I clamped my mouth shut around a gasp, their voices rose louder, with more recognizable words tangled between the unfamiliar ones.

"Stream like a current... from one source to another... like silt and flesh... Rise up and take hold."

Thomas reached toward Nolan Junior at the same moment that Marie did. They yanked the boy's body overtop of his grandfather, who was still fully submerged. Bubbles of breath were popping on the surface of the water.

Were they going to *drown* Nolan Senior? What the fuck?

But something in me already knew it wasn't that simple. The supernatural power in the air surged over us, and my skin crawled with horror I couldn't totally explain. I braced myself, my nerves jangling with the sense that any second now I'd need to fight for my life.

It wasn't my life on the line, though. All three of the adult Gauntts gave another shove and pushed both Nolans beneath the surface. They held them there, their voices rising and falling in a high-pitched wail that had no words at all.

Jett shuddered next to me. Nox let out a near-silent curse. Then, just when I'd have imagined even the boy was turning blue and sucking water into his lungs, they tugged him up again.

They brought out only him, hauling him to his feet

with much more gentleness than they'd displayed when sending him into the water, and helped him take wobbling steps onto the spit's higher ground. Nolan Senior didn't surface. As the other adults huddled around his grandson, it seemed as if they'd forgotten the patriarch altogether.

They'd stopped their wailing and their murmuring. There was a flurry of toweling off and the draping of a blanket I hadn't noticed they'd brought with them around the boy's shoulders. Marie touched the boy's cheek in an affectionate gesture that felt somehow not quite right from a woman to her grandson. But it was Thomas who spoke first.

"All okay in there, pops?" he said with a laugh as if he'd made a hilarious joke. Which he should have been making, talking like that to his own son.

But Nolan Junior tugged the blanket tighter around him and raised his chin at a haughty angle that looked far too familiar. Recognition clanged through me like an alarm bell before he even opened his mouth.

"It's unfortunate we had to make the transfer this early. It'll be half a decade before you can even justify having me in the office in any capacity." He shook his head with a tut of his tongue that sounded far too mature for his apparent age and glanced toward the water. "But good riddance to that failing body. You did well, getting me out here this quickly. I wouldn't have held out much longer. That witchy *bitch*."

The last words came out in a snarl. He was referring to me, I realized, and the attack I'd made on him, but that revelation was only a whisper beneath the deluge of horrified understanding washing over me.

Nolan Gauntt had been dying—because of me. So his family had brought him out here... to push his soul into his grandson's body, just as my guys had stolen new bodies of their own.

And not only that, they must have *always* been planning on using the boy that way. Nolan had said they'd made the transfer 'early,' as if it'd been scheduled for some later date. Holy fucking hell.

Shock rolled over me in waves. I was reeling so hard, the other possible implications rushing through my mind in a jumble, that I didn't notice that the Gauntts were now marching toward the foot of the spit until their feet rasped over the matted grass just a few paces away from us.

They might have walked right past us in the shadows, never knowing we were there. But we'd decided to wait until they left, not to back down completely. And the Skullbreakers must have been disturbed by what they'd seen too.

The guys leapt to their feet around me, their faces twisted with revulsion, and lunged at the Gauntts as one being.

twenty-five

Lily

A cry stuck in my throat. I sprang up in the wake of the guys' charge, not sure if they'd assumed I'd be right there with them, not even knowing who I'd want to aim my powers at now. Should I try to rip Nolan's new heart away from him in that child's body? But what if the child's soul hadn't quite been smothered, and there was still some way to bring Nolan Junior back? Who was the worst of the remaining adults—Marie or the parents who'd willingly sacrificed their son?

The frogs surged forward with me—dozens more than I'd realized had slipped out of the marsh to join us. The soft thunder of their hops bolstered my resolve. As the Gauntts spun around, I fixed my gaze on Marie. I knew for sure that she'd not only been instrumental in the spell tonight but also in molesting so many other kids. With a hiss through my teeth, I hurled all the energy I'd recovered since the last fight toward the thrum of her pulse.

But it didn't reach her. The Gauntts threw up their arms defensively with a crackle of energy whipping through the air. They must have conjured a broader, thicker wall of defense than they had against Nox's bullet before. The ones Jett fired now ricocheted off that section of air in rapid succession.

Kai and Nox slammed into the barrier and stumbled backward before their magic could affect our enemies. And all sense of Marie's blood snuffed out as my magic crashed into that wall and disintegrated.

The Gauntts drew closer together, backing away from us at the same time. The guys continued battering their magical shield every way they could, and I summoned a wave out of the lake to pummel them from above. At the sound of the roaring water, Thomas jerked his hands upward, and the wave splattered into another barrier above them.

The frogs flung themselves at the invisible wall too, with a chorus of hoarse croaks. Nolan—who had been Junior and now was Senior in essence?—eyed them and broke his taut expression just long enough to sputter a laugh.

"This is your army?" he sneered in a tone that sounded way too old for the childish voice that carried it. "Pathetic. We've been in charge here since before any of you were even *born*, and we'll still be long after you're dead."

"Fat chance," Nox snarled, and battered the transparent shield with his fists and the power he could drive from them. Dull thuds reverberated through the air.

We weren't going to break through it. I felt that in the weariness that gripped my lungs as I hurled as much of my own remaining power at the barrier as I could.

We'd already been weakened by two previous fights tonight. But the Gauntts were worn down from their soul transfer ritual too. With both of us exhausted, it didn't seem like either of us could overcome the other. They hadn't managed to do anything except fend us off.

Which meant that if we could catch them another time when they were weakened but we had our full strength, we should be able to crush them.

I clung on to that shred of hope and the thought of Marisol and Ruin back at the apartment, waiting for us. The longer the Gauntts kept us busy here, the more time there was for their lackeys to go after the most vulnerable members of our group.

"Let them go," I said to the guys with as much disdain as I could will into my voice. "We'll take care of them later." Maybe we'd even get a chance to do it right now after all if they let down their guards when we stopped our attacks.

Nox growled in defiance, but he stepped back half a pace, glaring at the Gauntts. Kai adjusted his glasses and nodded, easing farther back to flank me as Jett did the same. We watched the perverted supernatural family warily, braced to resume the fight at the first sign of trouble.

Nolan laughed again, and Marie squeezed his shoulder. A thread of nausea trickled through my stomach at a sudden thought. How many times had they done this before?

How many times had they shoved their souls into bodies that weren't theirs? How young had their previous hosts been? Melding their grown-up minds with the bodies of children… Was the blurring of the lines between child and adult what had warped their desires into something so disturbed when it came to other kids?

The possibility didn't make their behavior any less sickening. If anything, it was doubly horrifying that their awful ritual might have created something even more awful inside them, spreading the damage they did with their monstrous perversions all through the community around them.

I'd only had time to shudder at the thought when Nolan leapt forward with his arm stretching upward.

With a snapped word, he bounded off the ground and rammed his palm into Nox's face where the Skullbreakers boss was standing just a couple of steps ahead of the rest of us. We sprang at him, magic whining through the air, but Nolan already wrenched himself back to the safety of the shell that protected the entire family.

Nox fell. He crumpled like a rag doll, his legs giving

out under him, his head lolling backward. He'd have smacked his skull on the muddy ground if Jett and I hadn't caught him.

His eyelids dropped shut. His mouth gaped open. And his skin shone deathly pale around a nickel-sized blotch like a birthmark that now stained the middle of his forehead.

No! Every particle in my body screamed in refusal. First Ruin and now him?

"What the fuck did you do?" I shrieked, launching myself at the Gauntts again with a rush of panicked fury. I propelled my magic at them, groping for even one thread of blood I could sense through the barrier and throttle someone's heart with.

I felt their shield waver and maybe even crack—but then they were chanting again, hustling away from us. Nolan's mouth set in a creepy childish smirk.

I hesitated between charging after them and trying to help Nox, but my own legs felt ready to give beneath me. I sank down next to the Skullbreakers boss, staring at Kai, who'd dropped to his knees too. He was patting the larger guy's face with increasing urgency. Nox's muscles didn't so much as twitch.

The question wrenched of me. "Is he *dead*?"

Kai looked up at me with haunted eyes. "I don't know."

about the author

Eva Chase lives in Canada with her family. She loves stories both swoony and supernatural, and strong women and the men who appreciate them. Along with the Gang of Ghouls series, she is the author of the Bound to the Fae series, the Flirting with Monsters series, the Cursed Studies trilogy, the Royals of Villain Academy series, the Moriarty's Men series, the Looking Glass Curse trilogy, the Their Dark Valkyrie series, the Witch's Consorts series, the Dragon Shifter's Mates series, the Demons of Fame Romance series, the Legends Reborn trilogy, and the Alpha Project Psychic Romance series.

Connect with Eva online:
www.evachase.com
eva@evachase.com

Printed in Great Britain
by Amazon

32444054R00155